TIDE

JOHN KINSELLA

TIDE

JOHN KINSELLA

MELBOURNE, AUSTRALIA
www.transitlounge.com.au

First Published 2013
Transit Lounge Publishing

Front cover image: Philip Schubert
www.philipschubertphotography
Cover and book design: Peter Lo
Printed in Australia by McPherson's Printing Group

A cataloguing entry for this title is available from the
National Library of Australia: http://catalogue.nla.gov.au

ISBN: 978-1-921924-49-1

To Tracy, as always

The author wishes to acknowledge
the traditional owners and
custodians of the land he writes

CONTENTS

TIDE

The sea was gone, and the wet that filmed the mud was something else. It wasn't the sea, it was the bottom of the sea. But the sea was gone and the silver of the horizon was only light, a bright concentrated light full of sun and sky. It was the bottom of the sea and they were walking out over it, further and further out into its bubbling weirdness.

The two boys moved out from the fetid shade of the mangroves and made tentative steps into the wide-open expanse of the mudflats. They wore sandshoes because they knew about the sting of cobblers stranded in the mud, and then there were the great clawed mud crabs and even sea snakes that might have forgotten about the tide, floundering about. The smell was of salt and rot, and they thought the insides of mud crabs must be rotten, too. The mud bubbled and spat at them. Early in their walk, the mangroves that edged the beach wouldn't give up, and stuck up stems with growths on them that quickly crusted with salt in the harsh sun. Each step they took further out to the horizon, where the sea should be but wasn't, the thirstier they became.

Their shoes went thwock thwock in the mud. Sometimes they sank and stuck; other times the mud seemed as hard as a footpath and they almost skated over it, half running and stumbling. Each seemed to enjoy the other's successes but also to relish his difficulties. The older, taller one laughed loudest when the younger sank and couldn't pull his shoe out, the grey and black squirming around the bare ankle and sending its grit and ooze down around the foot, the toes. It was foul and strangely addictive. But they both tired fast, and when they stopped to look back at the mangroves' opaque, dark-green rigging, they felt even more tired. The green was starting to look like the horizon and the horizon started to make a ring, a halo.

The older boy said, We'll be in trouble when we get home.

The younger boy, marvelling at the breadth and volume of the sky, said, It'll be worth it when we reach the horizon.

The older boy smiled. He was half-proud of his little brother's wisdom. His little brother knew about nature, though he as the older one shouldered most of the blame and got into more trouble.

Occasionally the distance between them grew as the small boy lagged and the older one raced ahead, because he could. And just when the younger boy was on the verge of tears, the older boy would stand still and call out, Come on slowcoach, we're almost there!

No, we're not, said the small boy when he caught up. The horizon never gets closer.

Yes, it does, it's closer than when we left. Look back – the mangroves are like a mirage, and are turning into horizon. That means the horizon where the sea was has to be something we can reach.

The small boy, who was smart, listened to his brother's sophistry and believed only because he was excited to be out of the world he knew, and in this almost imaginary world where the unexpected and the unknown seemed part of the fabric of the eternal mudflats, the mundane repetition of each step. He was thirsty and tired, and shook his head in confusion. He wasn't sure what he was thinking. Only that though each step seemed the same, and the world looked the same with each step, that anything could happen. That sameness meant a surprise was inevitable. He sucked salt off his arm, making him both relieved and thirsty at once.

I wish we'd brought a drink, said the younger boy.

Yes, me too, said the older boy. I think we need to head back home, and come out tomorrow with some food and drink.

Yes, said the small boy. And a camera.

A camera? laughed the older boy. Why? There's nothing to photograph.

But there is! said the younger boy. It's *everything* out here.

What's everything? said the older boy, pushing his brother into the mud.

Don't! said the younger boy. That's mean. You always spoil things.

The older boy, feeling contrite enough to help his brother

from the mud, told him that his white T-shirt looked like a Collingwood footy jumper.

Does not! said the smaller boy, who did not barrack for Collingwood.

Hey, look! Where you fell over there's a crab flicking at the mud. Look at the size of its claws. The older brother kicked at the giant crab, and a steel claw latched onto the edge of his shoe. It didn't crush his toes because his shoes were a size too big (as were all his clothes – he would never accept the size he really was and demanded 'the next size up'), but it gave him a hell of a fright. Yow! Ouch! Hell, hell, hell! Bastard crab. He shook his shoe in the air but the crab wouldn't let go.

If you stop behaving like a clown, said the younger boy, and put your foot back on the mud, it will probably let go. It doesn't like you and probably wants to get away as much as you do.

The older boy, who had been dancing in the end because he liked the drama and watching his own foot performing its antics, suddenly stopped and put his foot down, and they watched the crab let go and submerge back into the mud.

It looked repulsive.

It was camouflaged.

I am so thirsty, said the younger boy. I'm going back. And with that he turned and started tracking his own footprints. He dared not go any other way because the mangroves truly were a horizon now.

The older boy stared at the sea horizon they'd been aiming for. As the sun dipped close to its surface, it looked like it was bleeding red. A red sea. He said, The sea is coming back. It's coming back fast.

The older boy ran past his brother, who was standing still,

looking at the sea covering his shoes. The horizon has broken, he said. We're in a bowl and the horizon is spilling into the centre.

Run, said the older brother. If we don't run, the tide will catch us and we'll drown.

The young boy, who was so smart, didn't really understand. This was a new experience. They'd only just moved to this far northern place where their father had gone after the divorce. Six months in the tropics, six months in the cold of the deep south. That horizon – the *water* – was rising so fast. He said, It wouldn't be like drowning. It would be as if the world had gone back to the way it always was.

Stop being a little idiot and run!

The small boy wondered about his brother far ahead. The water was around his knees, and he was tired and thirsty, and every step was a slow, struggling slosh slosh slosh. He wondered about the mud crabs. And the sea snakes would be coming back, the ones that hadn't been stranded. They have tails like oars and kill you quick. He couldn't see horizon in either direction now because horizon was all around him. It was dark and light and shaded and bright. It shimmered and stung his eyes. He kept walking, steadily, slosh slosh slosh.

He couldn't see his footprints from the journey out, but every now and again he glanced up at his brother, still far ahead. Slosh slosh slosh. The water was up at his waist and he swore that next time he would bring a bottle of water because you can't drink the sea. You're not *allowed* to drink the sea.

AFRICA REEF

Dylan had heard that it was called Africa Reef because it was halfway to Africa. It was a long way out to sea, out in the open ocean, a weird protrusion surrounded by deep waters. Maybe an island that hadn't yet formed, or had been swallowed by the waves. He wasn't sure, and when he asked he got no more than the usual story, though more often than not it was said 'halfway to bloody Africa'.

He did know, though, that this new town he was living in was on the 'shipwreck coast', where for hundreds of years ships had come to grief. And out at the Islands there had been mutiny and mass murder. The local museum was full of relics from the early days of European exploration and the watery graves of fate. With apprehension and excitement, he pieced this together in his head, making a narrative that compelled him to accept his new best friend's offer to visit Africa Reef, Saturday afternoon on his father's boat.

At least it compelled him to ask his mum, who rang his best friend's father and talked it over. After ascertaining that the father was a police sergeant and all passengers on his boat would wear life jackets, she gave a nervous, cautious 'okay'. Two former best friends of the sergeant's son would be shipping out as well. The boat would be back at the marina by dark, and they'd all be home soon after that. The weather was still warm and soothing.

The boys were all thirteen. Dylan was excited to be living in a new place, but the other boys were keen to leave their coastal town and go just about anywhere else. Eighteen miles out to sea, straight out into the wide ocean, certainly qualified as 'anywhere else', and though they considered themselves too old and too sophisticated to say they were embarking on an adventure, they all secretly felt that they were.

Dylan had just started reading *The Old Man and the Sea* for English, with his usual lack of enthusiasm, but now he decided to get stuck into it, as well as the book he'd seen on his gran's shelf, *The Cruel Sea*, though he knew nothing about that one and couldn't pronounce the author's name.

Dylan walked down to the beach every day after school and stared out long and hard, filling his head with the vastness. He had come from far inland where there was also vastness, but a vastness that was red and dry; or on those rare occasions when water came, it was a huge flood that vanished after a few days. But what the sea and the desert had in common was the immensity of the sky itself, arching over them like a protective dome, keeping things in and out, keeping and making secrets. The sky seemed to be the reason for the desert's existence, and for the sea's existence.

The police sergeant, with his son and the two other boys, collected Dylan from outside his house on Saturday after an early lunch. Dylan's mum had a quick, reassuring chat with the sergeant, and hugged her son, reminding him to be sensible and do what he was told. Normally Dylan would have been embarrassed, but he was too excited to care and the other boys were the same. One of them, Serge, whom Dylan knew least, scowled and smiled at the same time in a way that was ambiguous, but not ambiguous enough for Dylan to spend any time thinking about. And it was through the back window of the car, and Dylan's eyes were *really* on the twenty-foot boat that sat on the trailer behind the four-wheel drive. He'd seen it before, at his mate's place. It was called *Hilda*, after the sergeant's wife. It didn't seem that big, really, but it did have a large outboard motor – an Evinrude – on the back.

Once they reached the marina, the boys hopped out of the car so the sergeant could back the boat trailer down the ramp. His son directed him with precision, knowing his dad had little patience for showing off, especially when doing something serious. Once the trailer was submerged, the sergeant winched the boat down, down, down into the green water. Wading in up to his waist, he directed the boat around the ramp and, taking a rope hooked to the bow, dragged it to the small beach alongside. There were other craft, but since the sergeant was a well-known local, the other weekend sailors did their best to avoid him.

He called to the boys to hold the rope while he jumped in and got the sheet anchor, which he tossed into clear space on the shore and jumped out to secure. The boys, champing to get on the boat, held its bow while the sergeant parked the four-wheel drive and trailer exactly where they should be. Then the boys clambered on board. The sergeant retrieved the anchor and towed the boat out, then climbed aboard himself. He told his son to lower the outboard; then, just as the other boys thought they were drifting too close to the marina jetty, he started the engine and turned the boat out towards open sea. Dylan was overwhelmed as he sat with the others at the back – at the *stern* – watching the water churning and frothing, the propeller digging its furious, white wake.

As the boat skipped along past the grain ships moored outside the shipping lanes, Dylan considered the only way to confront, to absorb such vastness was in the orderly manner of the sergeant, who said nothing more than was necessary. Occasionally one of the other boys hooted with joy, but the sergeant's son was clearly on duty with his father, watching for any sign of a command, and if he was enjoying himself it was only in a form specific to his relationship with his father. The two former best friends, who were very close, pointed to the town they were leaving behind, muttering under their breath and barely restraining their excitement. They didn't invite Dylan into their conversation, which they directed over the engine's roar and the hull's slap slap slap on the gentle swell. Dylan didn't mind.

When Dylan noticed the waterspout on the horizon, he said nothing, because he didn't understand what it was. He was sure, though, that no-one else had seen it, because he had trained his eye to see so far into the distance, into the vastness, that he hardly believed anyone else could see that far or in that way. But the others did notice clouds forming on the horizon, and the sergeant half yelled above the boat-noise, Have to keep an eye on that, the weather comes up fast out here.

But he kept the boat going at a steady pace, and a half-hour passed before he spoke again.

That cloud's building and the wind is picking up, boys, so we might play it safe and head back in today. We can come out on another day.

The two former best friends moaned a little, but the sergeant's son cut them a look that said, Don't do it, my father's not in the mood.

Dylan wondered where the shore was. He considered the sun, which was fast vanishing behind thick cloud, and thought he'd worked it out. The boat was old, but had a compass and all the safety gear, and they all felt overprotected rugged up in their orange life jackets. The sergeant cut back on the throttle and curved the boat around.

Look, boys! he called. Dolphins.

His son, no longer able to restrain the excitement he'd been sitting on, burst out. Please, Dad, we're not going to see Africa Reef – can we just sit here for a few minutes and watch the dolphins?

The sergeant looked at the boys, all well-behaved, and said, Just for a few minutes. The sky's getting dark out there and it's coming in. We don't want to get caught.

And the boat was rocking much more than it had been, and with the engine idling, it started to tilt in ways it hadn't tilted before. The dolphins surfaced, submerged, surfaced, submerged, appeared a long way off, then vanished.

Okay, boys, said the sergeant, we're off. He pushed the throttle lever out of idle position and accelerated. The engine sputtered and died. He tried to restart, and it sputtered and died again. Another death later, he said gruffly, Move out of the way, boys, and went to check the fuel tank, and then the motor itself.

Enough fuel, he said, squeezing the bulb and checking the indicator. Motor doesn't smell flooded.

He messed with it a while, though he had trouble because the swell was gaining strength, tossing him and the boys together. Watch it, boys! he roared. Dylan retreated to the cabin area under the bow deck. The other boys followed him, except the sergeant's son, who was stationed at the wheel, holding on as if all life depended on it. Dylan felt a jab in his back, and looked around to see Serge snarling at him. Out of my way, you dork, he said just loud enough for Dylan alone to hear. You're a bloody stranger, mate, and if anyone's getting the comfy position it's not going to be you.

Dylan moved, and looked out at the sergeant, the dead motor, the vast sky black in all directions now. A strong wind was cutting across the boat and spinning it like a top. Every time the boat went side-on to the swell, it felt as if it was going to tip and capsize. Dylan rolled onto Serge, who openly thumped him and yelled to the sergeant, This guy's a dag, Sir, he's rolling onto me like a girl.

The sergeant yelled against the wind, Act like a man, son! Dylan knew the instruction was meant for him.

As the sergeant worked frantically at the motor, barking at his son to 'turn it over' every now and again, he began to swear. Fucking prick of a thing, fucking bastard. The fucking battery will be flat next and then we'll be well and truly fucked. The swell was getting massive and there was fear in everyone's eyes, even the angry sergeant's.

Then, on his father's instructions, the son turned the ignition again and the engine fired into life. The sergeant lurched to the wheel, pushed his son aside and said, Hold on, everyone! He faced the boat into the pitch of the waves and started towards the shore, rubbing the top of the boat's compass as if it were a talisman. He called to his son to look for the flares in the front of the boat, and have them ready.

Serge and the other boy were clinging to each other, then Serge vomited and vomited. Dylan noticed Serge had literally turned green, but he didn't find any satisfaction in it. He just stayed still and stared into the place where the sun should have been, where all life came from. He thought of the desert sun, the inland sun he'd grown up with. It could burn you alive in no time, but he missed it.

The sea had become the smallest place in existence: it wasn't vastness, just weight, crushing weight. It felt as if it was going to break through the hull at any time. Water was sloshing through the cabin. Soon, with the sergeant's son, he was working the bilge pump, unsure who had told him to do it or how he knew what to do, or even what it was. Serge looked like death, and Dylan feared him. The other boy held Serge tight and Dylan thought it'd be nice to have a friend who cared so much. He'd had friends like that out in the desert and yet had been to eager to leave them. To go somewhere, anywhere. Africa. Africa Reef. His friends had been closing in on him. He'd felt he was losing the key to the vastness, the space.

They broke through the edge of the storm, and the sea began slowly to settle. The sergeant looked at Serge's vomit but not at Serge. To his son he said simply, You can clean up that mess when we get home. Should have done it over the bloody side. There was shame everywhere. Dylan thought of saying, I'll help, but knew that it was better to say nothing. He wasn't trying to win friends, and he wasn't trying to make enemies.

When they'd got back to shore and had managed to hoist the boat up onto the trailer, Dylan wondered about Hilda, the sergeant's wife. He'd met her a few times and she was so beautiful and soft. He wondered how it would have all gone if *she'd* been on the boat, rather than just her name.

The sergeant spread plastic sheets over the seats of his car. He said to Serge, You should really walk home, but when Serge started off on trembling legs, covered in vomit and soaked to the skin, he called, I was joking! Before allowing the boys to get into the car, he said, Look out at the sea, boys. Never take it for granted.

And they did look. Dylan saw another waterspout, but as no-one mentioned it, he assumed that he alone could see it, and kept his mouth firmly shut. A new town, a new way of life. He pondered how the waterspout's grey-white reminded him of the dust devil's red-white swirl in the desert, spouts of dust joining desert and sky. And Dylan knew the sea and the sky had reasons for sharing or not sharing their secrets.

ORBIT

Two-stage rocket with capsule equals: two forty-four gallon drums, the side of a packing case, fencing wire, switches from an old country telephone exchange, wooden fruit boxes and a pram seat. A gantry made from fence pickets and nails, looking like a ladder but being so much more, and a blast area of grey sand with tufts of wild oats (green), with mission control (manned by a cardboard box, pineapple-tin-legged robot with red globes for eyes and two batteries series-circuited together for innards) the great brick and concrete shed his father used for servicing cars and trucks.

Launch time was straight after breakfast Saturday. Preparations had been over a couple of weeks, though no-one had noticed. His dad was away, maybe forever, and his mum had the baby to worry about.

He'd acquired a roll of tinfoil. Where is that foil? his mother had asked herself, not even glancing in his direction. Then the baby cried because it had 'done a nappy'. He needed the foil to protect him from the rays. Deflection. He went to his dad's rag bag in the shed and took as many as he thought he could get away with: insulation.

He knew the risks he was taking, but he was prepared. He'd given his mum an extra-big hug after his porridge, and she'd looked surprised. But there was no reason a cosmonaut couldn't show affection to his mother. It made him no less brave. He even tickled the baby under the chin and felt warm when it laughed. Irritating thing. But it was, after all, kin. His dad, well, he'd shake hands with him on his return, if either of them made it back. No point making a song and dance before something was done. When his father had injured his back in his fourth big-time league football match he'd said to his son, See, if I'd made a song and dance about getting in the team, I'd look ridiculous now. I'll never play again, son, never. I'm washed up before I've begun. But at least I didn't humiliate myself. His father had squeezed his hand so hard when he said this, the boy had almost cried. He would never cry, not even if he started burning up on re-entry. After all, the pain and fear wouldn't last long. It'd be over in an instant. What you don't know about won't hurt you. Don't cry over spilled milk. You've got to be in it to win it. The mantras followed him all the way to the launch site.

Scaling the gantry, he thought of the apricots just about ripen on the tree by the hedge. Don't eat too many of them, or you'll get collywobbles. He risked taking three or four. He also had a glass bottle in the capsule, in case he needed to take a piss. His pockets were sticky with wine gums he'd saved from his afterschool Friday treat. Space food.

He stepped into the capsule and pushed the gantry away. There'd be no going back. The countdown was at T minus five and counting. He closed the hatch with tinfoil and wedged some rags in around the gap between his seat and the foil. He stored his supplies. Settling in to the seat, he drew a strap across his waist. He pushed the motorbike helmet (cracked – a gift from an uncle after a near-fatal accident) over his head. He flicked the toggle switches in front of him, and ran through his checklist. There was a dodgy reading in the port thruster so he tapped a gauge. It came right. The Soviet space program had to make do with what they could dig up, but it usually came through. Solid, he reassured himself.

Then there was a moment of genuine alarm. A red light. A bell sounding. What was it? He pulled off his helmet to listen. It was his mother calling him from the back step. Gee, she was loud. He could hear her over the brooding engines. Once they ignited in a few minutes, tens of thousands of pounds of thrust would eviscerate the surrounding area. His mum could be irritating, and she was always crying or yelling, or cuddling him, but she was one of the reasons he was doing this. She needed to know that at least one of her men could make good, would leave and return a better person. She would be proud of him. She was calling, Come to the phone, your cousins want to know if you'd like to go for a swim. Where are you?

And then she was gone. He was always vanishing. He was always wandering down to the beach. He wasn't allowed to swim on his own, but he was allowed to pick up shells and make sandcastles and wander the shore. He liked that. They weren't too far away. And he'd learnt to swim early. He was the best swimmer in the world for his age. He could swim the entire Indian Ocean if he needed to. He could rescue a full-grown man from the breakers which smashed incessantly on the beach, filling his ears and his bedroom endlessly. He looked forward to the silence of space. The vacuum. His mother had been a swimming teacher and though she lived by the sea she was always saying to his dad, I wish we had a pool, I could give lessons. Don't be daft, woman, he'd say, we've got half the world's water on our doorstep. You can't teach lessons in surf, she'd say.

The ocean was central to his plan. After re-entering the earth's atmosphere, he'd splash down just beyond the breakers and surf his way in. The beach was deserted at this time of year so he wouldn't get busted or land on anyone. True, there'd be no witnesses, other than the gulls and the dolphins, but *he'd* know, and his mother would believe him. She always believed him. And she'd tell Dad, and if he didn't believe, Mum would insist and he'd either believe or leave again. How many times had he left? This time, though, he said, I'll be fucked if I'm coming back! Don't swear in front of the boy, she'd cried. But the boy knew every swearword. The boy knew every word that'd ever been written or said. He knew why he was on earth. He had a purpose. He had a mission.

Helmet back on, he continued the check. T minus two and counting. The engines were hotting up and the whole launch vehicle began shaking. Just for a second, he wondered if it'd hold together, if he hadn't been a little hasty joining the two stages. He was briefly concerned for the *integrity of the vehicle*. But it was too late for doubts.

FLIGHT

We met him under the wharf. We were drinking Brandivino, and he asked for a swig. We didn't mind because he was about ten years older than us, and we figured we could make use of him for a bottle-shop run. I was the eldest of our trio, about three months short of my eighteenth birthday. He also cadged a couple of cigarettes off us, smoking them cupped in his hand because the draught swirls down there, coming in between the ships and the pylons.

He crouched on the narrow gangway and rocked back and forth. If it'd been night we probably would have been a little scared of him: filthy, in an army surplus greatcoat, matted hair becoming dreadlocks, a crazed beard, and eyes that burnt somewhere between brown and grey. He didn't speak much but when he did it was kind of forceful – emphatic.

And then he almost knocked us from our tenuous perches over the surging green water. He said, I can fly.

It was the way he said it. We knew straight away that he didn't mean he could fly in a plane, or even fly a plane, or hang-glide or paraglide or perform any other assisted method of flight. In his eyes he said it as well: he could fly!

We believed him the moment we perceived what he was saying. Immediately. We saw it simultaneously in our slightly buzzed collective mind's eye. Under that greatcoat we knew he had the wings of an angel or a devil, or both.

We asked if he could fly for us. For us to see – to witness.

He was a funny bugger. Not under here, he said, I am not as small as those swallows darting in and out of the pylons.

We all laughed, and took deep swigs, and thought about the bottle ending soon. We handed him the last drop as a gesture of solidarity and goodwill.

If we give you the money, will you pick up another couple of bottles from the pub down the road? Sure, he said. Not a problem. And we all hauled ourselves from the watery underworld of below-wharf, and climbed the steel ladder facing the sea, up into the above-wharf light. It was actually a warm day, though you wouldn't have known it below-wharf. The sun had a pleasant heat to it. Gulls and terns wheeled overhead, and a sailor on the stern of a ship moored alongside the wharf watched a large gob of his spittle fall far down to the sea. You could imagine small fish rising to the bait. I've seen that happen before. Maybe that's what the sailor was doing – amusing himself in a time-honoured way.

Will you fly after we've got more grog? we asked.

I will, he said, though after I fly I will have to leave town.

No community tolerates me being among them once they've seen me fly. Once airborne I soar high and always attract attention.

~

I first thought I could fly when I was six. Not in that run-of-the-mill Superman-off-the-shed-roof way, but literally. It started in my dreams – I would fall off a mountain and be crashing to earth, and then I'd pull up just before impact and find myself soaring towards treetops and clouds. Then a few years later I was standing on the beach and saw what I thought was a shark fin, and my sisters were swimming and not looking. I called to them and they couldn't hear, and the fin was getting closer. I just crouched and leapt into the air, and then I was flying over the waters and plunged down at the fin and splashed the water and the shark snapped at the air, missing me, and I drove it out to sea and then flew back to the shore. My sisters said nothing. No-one said anything and the day at the beach went on as before.

~

Last week I had sex with a girl I've been lusting after for a year. I think I really like her. We went to the Year 12 ball together but nothing happened. Most of our classmates went down to the city for university but we both stayed on here, planning to head down in a year or two. My close mates had all left school at fifteen and got work on the cray boats or on farms, and I wanted to be around them, drinking and partying. We kind of had a band going as well, so maybe that was it. Anyway, I've been in town and still drinking with my mates on weekends. They wanted every gory detail of what went on with Alice, and I told them. Our new below-wharf friend looked uncomfortable and kind of lagged behind as we made a beeline for the pub. But I could tell he was still listening.

∞

An orgasm isn't flying.

∞

Okay, he said, give me your money and wait down the street. He went in and came straight out with two bottles. He gave us the change. He knew how to win trust. Or maybe he was just trustworthy. Let's go and drink in the park by the Moreton Bay fig, one of my mates suggested. Yes, good launching spaces there, we laughed. Our new friend followed.

Under the Moreton Bay fig is an old roundabout – a merry-go-round you push yourself. When our friend plonked himself on the boards, two little children leapt off and ran away to their mothers on the thin harbour beach. He laughed uncomfortably, Kids do that. Must be the hair, he said. We laughed again. We were laughing a lot and looking to each other, excluding him more by doing so. We climbed onto the merry-go-round and propelled it with our feet, swigging and getting giddy, and risking losing the bottles which went from hand to hand. Drinking fast, we got pissed quick. The children came back with their mothers, who told us to get off and act our age. Especially you, mate, they said to our friend. One mother said to the other, Christ, he stinks to high heaven.

We laughed again – even our friend laughed – and we found a patch of grass bordering the beach, where we smoked and finished the grog. Now, will you fly? we asked. Give the kids and their old dears a treat!

⁓

Flying is intuitive, but to make good use of it takes time and craft. It's an art form, a skill. We can all fly. Yet we not only don't choose to – we rarely, if ever, attempt it. The risks of crashing, of losing control, are so great. But falling is the most important part of flying – its heart, and very likely its soul.

⁓

Do you need a run-up? someone joked.

No, it's from a standing start.

You're a helicopter!

Or one of those VTO military aircraft – a vertical take-off jet. A jump jet!

We cacked ourselves, but he didn't seem fazed. He just said, I don't like the military. It is an abuse of flying to use it to hurt people.

We weren't sure what to say, but offered him another cigarette, which he took.

So, I said, to break the ice, it's a gift …? Like some people can read minds, or bend spoons?

No, he said.

He was sitting in front of me, and the sun was low in the sky behind him. He was burnt into the sea, like a shadow puppet. I have to admit, it really looked like he had a halo. But he still stank. And I mean *stank*. I was pretty sure he'd shat himself, and the other guys thought the same, I could tell.

One of the mothers walked past to pick up her towel and gear from nearby. She'd been keeping an eye on it and the kids, and on our friend. I hadn't noticed till then but she was almost hot-looking – for a mum. She bent over, her arse towards us, shook her towel more than it needed shaking, folded and packed it into her bag, stretched, then walked really close to whisper something in our friend's ear.

He didn't move. Then she added, And you really do stink. She flicked us a look, and went off with her kids.

What did she say? What did she say? Come on, tell us!

Nothing, really. It's not important, he said.

We're all mates here. Come on, we'd tell you!

He rocked in and out of the sea, the sun. Gulls arced over his head and called violently into the sea breeze, which was picking up.

She said, *I know, I've seen you.*

What does that mean? Come on!

It means she has seen me fly somewhere. Maybe another town. Maybe she was one of a crowd who made me leave, move on to the next town. Maybe she's the vanguard. Maybe she's an avenging …

… angel?! we said stupidly. We were really pissed.

No, no angels. It's nothing to do with angels. They're mythic, and such an idea would be delusional, he said.

∞

I was a very practical youth. I only ever flew when necessary. I got out of practice quickly. I had other things to do. Landings are difficult at the best of times, but when your hormones are, as they say, raging, a landing is just dangerous. What's more, my mother went through a religious crisis, and bundled us off to Sunday school and church services every weekend, and even after school some days. That short-circuited my flying urge, as well as my flying abilities. Scripture convinced me there was no point in flying, and almost convinced me that I couldn't fly – even that I had never flown at all. Deep down, I knew this was rubbish, but the mind will believe what it wants, and, sadly, what is drummed into it.

Then my mum lost God as fast as she'd found Him, and I had total recall. But I still remained hesitant. The first flight after such a long break was actually painful. I ached for a week and could barely eat. I developed a fever of 108 and almost died, cooked from the soul out. When I was well again, my mother decided we'd move to a different state, and we packed up and I flew in a plane for the first time. It was like being on the ground. Looking out the window was like watching television. It's a fraud, a hoax.

∞

He was either going to fly or he wasn't. There was nothing

more we could do or say to make it happen. We just waited.

Then he said, or intoned, Launching from low places, and sea level is the epitome, it is as interesting as from high places. Though falling is not part of the take-off, of course, and that's a negative. But the kindling of will-power, the sheer energy to launch, is more than compensation.

My mates were silent – which is a rare thing. Transfixed on this filthy vagrant who'd found us under the wharf and made the afternoon pass faster than any afternoon of our lives. Even the grog had worn off, and we were much higher than it could ever have made us. Then I realised I'd not even asked him a thing about his life. How did he survive? Had he worked? He was what my mother called 'well-spoken', if a bit ragged around the verbal edges. And he had a way of being in your head without being invasive, of hanging around without being intrusive. I could learn from this guy, and so could my mates.

I could see they were thinking the same thing. After all, we'd stayed in town, but the action was four hundred k's down the coast, and maybe much further away than that. What kept me in town, really, what kept me – us – from flying? My mind was racing as I fixed on his silhouette, the sun now setting.

And then he was gone. He'd flown. I can't tell you how it happened, or what happened. I barely remember, or don't remember at all. I was lost in my thoughts, gazing, gazing, gazing, and then when I snapped to, he was gone.

Did he walk off? I asked my mates. I was annoyed.

What? Uh? Na … nup. No. They were as bemused as I was.

He was there. I was watching him. He didn't walk anywhere. He just wasn't there. Did he fly?

Flight is elevation. That's a truism. Mostly, rather than soaring through the firmament, ranging the globe, I hover – I tread water in the sky, hang in the air. Strangely, I've never been much of a swimmer and am not fond of the water. Some of you might blame the shark and my sisters, but I don't. I just don't like the sensation of liquid on my skin. I like air. I try to avoid flying in rain, though I will if needs be. But then, clouds are a different thing. The water vapour clings rather than washes. And I want all my sins, all my positives, to stick to my skin. I carry them with me and would not like to think they'd spill down over those I fly above. It's a gross thought. Each flight is a tattoo, speech written into my skin. The silence is a book of flesh. Sun, 'look not so fierce on me'! It burns to fly. Though I cannot help myself.

She's only eight years older than me. Her kid is five. We're driving all the way to Sydney, the other side of the country. Four thousand kilometres from here. My mates have already left. One is in London working in a pub – his dream, he tells me – and the other is at TAFE in Perth. I'd like to tell you I am training to be a pilot, but I am not remotely interested. Flying in a plane is not flying at all.

When I saw her downtown one day, I had to ask. I said,

41

You won't remember me …

I do, she said.

You whispered something in his ear, before you insulted him. What was it?

I said to him, 'Faustus is gone. Regard his hellish fall …'

What on earth does that mean? I asked. And she said, Fuck me and you'll *fly*.

Terminat hora diem; terminat auctor opus.

DUMPERS

On Long Beach, which ran down one side of the peninsula town, the waves were considered temperamental. Serious surfers rarely bothered, but beginners mingled with bodysurfers and boogie-boarders most days whether the surf was 'pumping' or not. It was a wind-driven shore break, without a spot of reef around, so the direction of the wind made all the difference to the shape of the waves. And when it wasn't 'working', Long Beach was a washing machine, a grind of foam and sand and crushing dumpers. It was also notorious for savage rips that would cart swimmers way out into the bay and then on to deep ocean. You would never call it a family beach, but nonetheless families wandered down over the dunes and spent whole days there on weekends. During the week, other than a few kids wagging school and the odd neophyte surfer willing to take on anything, it was pretty well deserted.

But during the warmest weeks of the school year, the senior sports master, Mr Rush, would walk his upper-school students across the dunes to Long Beach for 'beach activities'. This would include swimming if the water was considered 'safe' enough, as well as beach cricket and volleyball. For two hours on a Thursday afternoon, the Pacific gulls and seagulls would vie with Mr Rush's whistle for attention.

It was difficult to get inside Mr Rush's head. From outside, he seemed a brutal and brutalising man. A Korean War veteran who, though nearing retirement, was in perfect shape, with the body of a man twenty years younger, he unsurprisingly encouraged and protected his sports stars, and was harsh with the failures. He would turn a blind eye to hazing, and would laugh with his stars about the pathetic flailing of the 'weaklings'. Yet there was more to him than this, and even the weaklings who suffered under his reign knew it, and feared him all the more for it.

Some of them suspected he despised the stars even more than he despised *them*. They couldn't say how or why. It was something to do with the way he stared at them, looked at them when the stars weren't around; the occasional impatient gesture of hand lifting from hip to indicate something was *almost* right.

Andy Bright was one of the 'weaklings'. Because he was mediocre at his studies, but capable of being top of the class if motivated enough, he was nicknamed Brighty. Maybe they would have called him Brighty anyway. It seems the default setting. Though not a total failure at sports, he wasn't well-built and was a late developer, that greatest sin among boys. But if he liked a sport he could do well enough to avoid a pummelling from the 'stars', who might still grab his balls in the changing rooms where he tried to change under a towel close to the door (escape hatch) as quickly as possible.

On one occasion Dag and Mutt, the two star full-forwards of the school, had dragged him out of the change rooms semi-naked and dumped him in front of the girls' change rooms, watching as he writhed in humiliation. The girls didn't actually laugh much, though Mr Rush grabbed him by the ear and dragged him back. That was justice Mr Rush–style.

However, Brighty didn't mind sports on beach days, finding he could run around a bit, splash a bit, and generally muck around under the radar with the other weaklings. Mr Rush wasn't such a hardnut on beach days, though you wouldn't think this if you walked past. He still blew his whistle insanely and yelled abuse at boys who were faltering. You'd also notice his crew cut, the zinc cream on his face like war paint, the shorts so tight it was clear he'd carefully arranged his prominent 'bits'. On the beach he took his shorts off like all the boys, and across his back was a tattoo that said *Mum*. Years earlier, when one of the sporty boys had joked with Mr Rush about this, the consequences had been so extreme that the legend kept in check whatever people even half thought about it. It was never mentioned.

Hey, Brighty, catch this!

Brighty turned round and caught a sand-ball right in the face. Mutt laughed, calling to Dag to come and look at Brighty trying to get the sand out of his eyes.

Some of the other boys laughed. Brighty laughed as well
– best method of defence – and plunged into the surf to get
the sand out of his hair. Since it was grinding hard that day,
he got more sand *in* than out. Because it was rough, the boys
had been told to stay within five metres of the shore. On
a perfect day, the waves would break right and occasionally
form crystalline green tubes, but today they were tumbling
head over heels and breaking at irregular points along their
crests. It was a mess. The wind was switching directions and
the sand on the beach occasionally flew into hair and eyes
anyway. Brighty wasn't worried.

He heard Dag calling to Mutt, Go out and give the
scrawny little bastard a dunking.

Even that didn't worry Brighty. Though he was small, he
was a good swimmer. Not a certificate-good swimmer, but an
untrained sort of swimmer, very familiar with the ocean and
with Long Beach in particular. He knew its moods. His older
brother Ben was a shit-hot surfer. A school drop-out, jobless
and into pot, he was another reason Brighty copped it from
the sports stars. His brother was a well-known 'lost-cause'.
But he could surf, really surf. Sometimes he took Brighty out
with him when Long Beach was working. Brighty had a long
plank of a board, and could only just stand up, but he always
enjoyed himself.

Go on Mutt, get out after him! Dag was getting frantic.

Brighty moved a little further out, just in case. He kept
one eye on Mr Rush, who would eat him alive for going out
that far, but Mr Rush had combined whistling and playing
and joined in the volleyball. Brighty thought Mr Rush looked
like he was having heaps of fun.

Then Mutt was running into the surf and lurching straight for him.

Brighty watched him approach. He could study Mutt closely because time had slowed down. Mutt was a handsome beast. A good six-four, sculpted muscles, already a few curls of black hair on his broad chest. And Mutt wasn't stupid, though he pretended to be. He was a top maths student, although a bottom English student. Mutt wore pink boardshorts because he could get away with wearing pink boardshorts. No-one was going to call *him* a poof.

The afternoon sun cast a halo in the spray around his hair as Mutt splashed and furrowed his way through the surf to where Brighty was treading water, bobbing among the dumpers. Brighty was ducking down as each dumper closed over, and managing to stay out of the washing machine. That was years of practice.

Mutt was close to Brighty now, but a dumper closed over him and sent arms and limbs flailing. Mutt emerged coughing and spluttering and angry. He staggered back to shore to find Dag laughing at him.

Get the little bastard, Mutt, get out there! And Mutt went back for more and got dumped again.

Brighty hung out just beyond the break. He kept an eye on Mr Rush, who was still too absorbed in spiking the volleyball into one of the student's legs to notice anything. Mr Rush was in a state of bliss.

Then suddenly Mutt was out near Brighty again. He'd snagged a break in the dumpers and got through, and was flailing at Brighty, who swam deftly out a few more strokes. Brighty felt the cold, then the pull of the rip, instantly. He was just on the edge of it and drew away just in time. But Mutt went straight into its throat. Within seconds he was being dragged out to deep water. He was tired from struggling with the dumpers, and Brighty could see that Mutt wasn't a strong swimmer. Muscle, but no savvy. Mutt was drowning.

Brighty didn't hesitate: he swam into the mouth of the rip. I am Jonah, he told himself. He was afraid but hyped, and swam with the rip until he reached Mutt. Next to Mutt he felt tiny. He felt his cock and balls shrivel even smaller as he collided with the school giant.

Grab my arm, Mutt. Brighty was going to sidestroke his way across the rip. Mutt was gurgling and flailing, and his wheeling arms struck Brighty so hard that they momentarily stunned him. They went out further with the rip, and Brighty himself started to swallow water and choke. Mutt was big and heavy and dragging him down. He was trying to climb on Brighty and use him as a liferaft. Brighty pushed him off and ducked under to grab Mutt around the neck and shoulders. Just lie on your back and kick your feet, Mutt!

Then Mutt gave way and his body relaxed, and he went with Brighty.

Exhausted, Brighty lifted his head out of the water as they broke the edge of the rip and saw all the kids standing at the edge of the surf. Mr Rush was there, blowing his whistle and pointing out to sea. By the time Brighty had dragged Mutt to the dumpers, Mr Rush was in there too. The dumpers broke around Mr Rush as if he were ancient granite that had been bashed and battered by waves for thousands of years. He wrested Mutt from Brighty and said, You'll make it back in from here, son. With that, he took Mutt the rest of the way to shore, where he gave him mouth-to-mouth.

Mutt was okay. Just sheepish. Not even Dag risked a joke. The class trudged back over the dunes to the school with Brighty dragging behind. No-one had said a word to him. They steered clear. He repelled them.

Back at school, Brighty walked carefully into the changeroom. He passed Dag, who had flung Brighty's bag across the floor.

Don't say anything about Mutt to anyone, you little bitch!

Brighty grabbed his bag and went to his place near the door, where he changed under his towel. He flinched, waiting for one of the stars to rip it away. Mr Rush had taken Mutt to the nurse's room, but everyone knew Mutt was fine. That was just the rules.

And then, when Brighty was walking away from the changeroom and from the day, he heard Mr Rush's whistle.

Hey Bright, I want a word with you.

He stood and waited because Mr Rush was coming to him. Mr Rush said, You learn in your life that some things never happen, son. No-one will thank you. No-one will say jack shit if you keep your mouth shut. And that's the best way, son. The best way. That's the pain – the pain of bottling it up – that'll keep you going. Get you up day after day ready to start again. You'll never shine on the field – never. Matt will, because he's a star.

Brighty watched Mr Rush walk crisply back towards his fiefdom. There was a heap of homework due in the next day, and he thought about heading over to the library. But then he kicked at the ground and thought, Nah … think I'll go hang out with my brother. He's always good for a laugh when he's stoned. And he won't be doing much else today – the surf's shit.

DIVE

The stretch of beach in front of the pioneer stone church bore the church's name, or the name of a saint. The old name was still known, but wasn't on the maps you find in service stations, nor on the lips of most parishioners.

The girl hiding behind a great Norfolk pine planted in the late nineteenth century, on a grassy knoll before the gentle sandhills that led down to the beach, was also named after a saint. She was the minister's daughter, and both boys wanted her.

The boys were down on the beach, and she could only just see their heads over the gentle undulations. At least, she thought it was them. They were there most afternoons. That was their 'dive spot'. They'd leave their towels and bags there. She'd known them both for ages but only this term, since she'd found they were in the same form class at school, had she started speaking with them. They smirked at her for being the minister's daughter. Bet you're a virgin, the nastier one had said straight out. Tight as! She thought he was likely a virgin too. Boys! They weren't even worth being interested in. She knew heaps of boys from her church.

She was the lady of the church, her father would joke. Her mother was long gone. One older lady had clashed with her father, and called across the car park, You're as snooty as that little bitch of a princess you've raised. It was rare to hear such talk anywhere near the church, and especially from one of her father's flock! She knew that one of the dive boys had never been to church, and the other had left church because of her father. She'd always ignored *him*. And he was too shy to say boo to a goose. Though he was brave enough to say, indignantly, Your dad doesn't know the difference between God and a cash register.

The ocean was choppy black-blue, and kelp had banked on the glaringly white sand, with subtle crescents of pink and grey. It'd been picked over by beachcombers that morning after the storm, and only the odd shell spiralled towards the sun. The water was still stirred up and murky. But the boys dived anyway.

Before they waded in – duck-walking in their flippers, swivelling at the hips to counter the lead on their weight-belts, masks on their heads like sunnies, gidgies with trident heads unstoppered and poised – one said to the other, I bet by the time we're back on the beach she'll be sitting by our stuff, reading a book.

Nah, not today, said the other, suddenly awkward with his gidgie, trying to pull his mask off, spit on the glass, and rinse in the ocean all at once.

Why not? asked his mate mockingly, as was his manner.

Because you said that stuff to her yesterday at school. Girls don't like hearing that sort of stuff. If I said that to my sister, she'd clout me one.

The other boy, only slightly larger, burst out laughing. If you said that to your sister, it'd be called incest, you weird little prick!

They were best friends. Always had been. But it was also a default setting: familiarity brought them together, and the fact that their parents were friends and let the boys be more 'independent' if they were independent as a pair … The theory being that one would keep an eye out for the other; that it would give them mutual checks and balances. That was the way the families talked. Both sets of parents were teachers. Social studies, social studies, maths and English. In a coastal town a long way from the big city down south, they made an effort to keep up the quality of conversation.

Yeah, right!

It was so murky they didn't stay out long. One of them had speared a blowfish, and gingerly waved it above the surface as a reminder of great trophy claims made on previous dives, but the murk beneath and the fact that when they were on the surface peering down, the chop drowned their snorkels and they swallowed buckets of seawater, decided them: no great victories or discoveries would be made that day. It was getting rougher and dangerous, and the girl would probably be there by now.

'Ow ya goin? they asked, as she sat with her knees to her chest and her dress tucked between her legs. They tried to peek but nothing was showing.

Oh, okay, she said. Find any shipwrecks?

Nah, too rough. It's a bugger out there. Can't see a thing.

She looked at them peeling off their half wetsuits and smiled. She thought, If I pull a face, it'll make them do something. Something show-offy or silly. Boys aren't very complex. She toyed with the idea but let it go for the time being. The sand was getting in her eyes.

What about Mr R telling us to take a night or two off our homework every week and get a life? she said.

Our parents reckon he's in for it, saying that. They work with him, and they say he was 'speaking out of turn'. But good on him!

Yeah, we said, 'If you make a fuss for him we'll tell all the family secrets to the other kids at school!'

You have family secrets? she asked, pulling her long, sun-bleached hair out of her eyes and mouth, trying to steady it and still pin her clothes in a non-provocative way as the wind churned the sand.

Nah, not really. Mind you, said the larger boy, punching his mate in the arm so he winced, but only just, I think there might be a few incest secrets in some closets. The punched boy blushed, and tried changing the subject by harping on his pet topic. How can you stand having people you know coming to your house to whinge to your dad about their personal problems?

Is your dad a minister or a sex therapist? the other boy quipped.

The girl shifted uncomfortably. It was always silly talk about sex. She probably wouldn't come down to the beach again when they were there. But it was her front yard. It was where she lived. She considered it *her* beach. The look she'd held back came over her face, and she said with something much more cunning and loaded than a smirk, I've got a surprise for whichever one of you can bring me the best treasure from the bottom of the sea.

Piss off, they said. Wouldn't go out in that mess again. And you're just a tease. You wouldn't give anything. We know your sort.

Bit like your sister!

This was followed by an awkward silence until the *slightly* smaller boy said, I don't mind having a go. Not for you, just for something to do. I bet I can come up with a neat shell or an old bottle or something. I know where everything is out there. I could find stuff in the dark.

And then he was pulling his gear back on and, leaving his gidgie behind, waddling down the beach and into the choppy grey. The other boy hopped after him, not even looking back at the girl. He flapped over, breathless, and whispered. I reckon she's hot for it. She'll really give us something.

What? asked the other boy nervously.

I dunno. Maybe she'll suck us off, or let us muff-dive her.

Muff-dive?

It's called a muff-dive when you go down below on a girl. You know, lick her out.

The slightly smaller boy shuddered involuntarily and said, Well, I don't really care about that, I just like a challenge. And with that he was into the ocean.

The surviving boy stood next to the girl, their heads lowered, surrounded by adults, listening to her father, the minister, give a eulogy. He praised the surviving boy for trying to drag his mate out from below the ledge of reef that had trapped him, reaching for something invisible. He praised his own daughter for raising the alarm when she understood what was going on. He praised police divers for recovering the body in such dangerous conditions. He didn't condemn the parents for anything. He got the measure of his town with his best homiletics experience. He delivered the right eulogy and the right sermon in the right way. Jesus' eyes remained lowered on the cross, and didn't glance up once in surprise or disappointment.

When they were alone, the boy said to the girl, He pulled me away when I was reaching in. I knew there was an old bottle in there, covered in barnacles and worms. I saw it weeks ago but went after a silver snapper that flashed past, and thought I'd go back some time. You couldn't see a thing down there. It was all feel. He was with me every stroke. And then he was past me and in too deep. I tried to pull him out, but I guess he thought I was trying to stop him getting whatever treasure might be in there. Deeper and deeper and then he was stuck. All the air rushed out. Even in the murk I could see the huge bubbles of escaping breath come out then they were smashed into millions of smaller ones. His legs flapped like crazy.

She kept her eyes down and listened to the sea rolling over the reefs and across the sand shoals on to the beach. The sea was loud despite it being a calm day with blue skies. But the small waves echoed and reverberated over the dunes, through the Norfolk pines, around the limestone of the church. The walls seemed so porous, the sea right in there with her, with them all. She listened to the floating calls of the gulls and tried to remember if there'd been any gulls on that day. She couldn't recall any, which was strange because they were always there, no matter the weather. But it seemed strong in her mind now that there was an absence of gulls. They abandoned the place.

Through the drone of her father, and the adults' tears, and the ocean's vexing roar, she stuck her hand out to one side, searching for *his*, but he pulled back and said, Sorry, I can't touch anyone. He was always bigger and stronger than me. He always showed me the way. He taught me things. He taught me about girls. I looked up to him.

FLARE

It's all in the packing of the powder, he told her.

What do you mean?

Well, you might think the rocket is just this tube full of gunpowder, but it's really how you put the gunpowder in the tube that makes it fly. Plus, I've got some extra-special accelerants mixed in with the gunpowder to make it burn fast and hot. Some aluminium powder, some magnesium, some oxidants. It'll light up like the sun.

In the god's chariot crossing the sky!

Precisely. That's why he loved her, wanted to impress her. She was literary and smart. He considered her a gem in that philistine seaside town. She quoted poems and never talked about clothes or pop singers. The other girls were wary around her. He'd loved her for four years of high school. They were Year Elevens now and just turning sixteen. He had never tried to kiss her, and she had never shown any inclination for being kissed.

They were alone in the shed. She sat on a bench dangling her legs, watching him work. Have you thought about what you'll do after the exams next year? Do you still want to study chemistry at UWA?

Yeah, I guess so. But you know that. Why are you asking again? He stopped packing the rocket and looked at her carefully. He had gunpowder on his hands and was breathing it in.

No reason, she said. Well, I don't know. I'm thinking I won't go anywhere. I might just stay here. She had somehow drawn her legs up and was perched on the edge of the bench, fine and delicate like a displaced songbird.

Why? he exclaimed, dropping the rocket; the carefully packed powder broke its sculpted form and spilled out of the casing. He'd been relying on her going to UWA. On her staying in the women's residency college while he was in the men's one nearby. Then it would all come together. Science and the arts. Life.

I can read books just as easily here.

He laughed, barely able to contain a snide put-down (he'd been working on that side of his 'personality' for her). What books? This town only sells romances and thrillers in the newsagency!

Oh, I can get books when we go down to Perth. My sister's moving there. I'd visit. I think I'll try for a job in the shire offices, and that'd give me money for books.

Where will you live?

At home.

At home! He could barely contain himself. Home? You've always wanted to get away from home. You call your parents 'philistines' more than I call this town a dump. It's your favourite word.

That's because I'm selfish and arrogant. That's not what it's about. My parents love me and want me at home for a few more years. I don't mind. I can read and write. They might not get it, but they don't stop me.

But your mother is always yelling at you, I can hear it from here. Their houses were separated by a vacant, partially bush-covered block, where he would occasionally blow things up, and her parents would speak to his parents and they would all threaten to tell the police.

Well, I can't wait to get away from home! His blood was heating, he was growing flushed. He loved her, but love doesn't work if everything else isn't right. He'd mapped it all out. He'd been waiting to make his move and now everything was stuffed up. For years he'd endured taunts from boys at school about his 'doin' her on the vacant block' and from the other girls for being a 'poof and not being able to get it up'. He was called the Professor after the nitwit on *Gilligan's Island* who was frustrated and clammed up. Who didn't even get it off with Mary Ann properly, never mind Ginger. He'd bided his time. There had to be a pay-off.

The shed – the lab – went silent. She'd eased back into her former position on the bench, with legs dangling and swinging; it irritated him. He felt scrunched-up in his abdomen and a small amount of sick came into his mouth. He went back to the rocket and started packing it hard, really hard. He crammed more and more powder into the tube, damaging the cone and fins.

It won't fly properly if you don't fix those, she said.

He straightened them out roughly, put the rocket in a plastic bag and said, Come on.

There was a block, then the coastal road, and a set of railway tracks before they reached the breakwater. Over recent years the beach had been filled in with large chunks of limestone to shore it up against the tail end of cyclones. One reached the town every few years, churning the place up and tearing away at the land's innards, sucking them out into the water.

As they walked down in silence, the rocket cradled in his arms, they kept their eyes fixed on the ocean. There was always the ocean. If she dropped out of sight for a few days, or he went to sulk, they'd inevitably reconnect on the rocks, the spray splashing up over them even on still, fine days. The limestone chunks had not yet been smoothed by the sea; they shattered the slightest wave to droplets and foam. The two of them tasted of salt. They knew each other's taste by the sea's taste spread through the air.

Crossing the rail lines that fed the port, she said, We're all elemental, you know.

Maybe.

We are.

There's a slight sea breeze, he said, wanting to reach across her face and lift a strand of hair that had drawn across her eye, her nose and her opposite cheek. He wanted to put her face in order. But he never touched her. Ever.

It's a pleasant breeze, though, she said.

It's okay, but it would be better if it were a still day. The breeze will mess with the flight path. I'll aim it straight out to sea instead of up.

He'd already scouted a suitable launch site, and hidden a length of aluminium drainpipe in the culvert alongside the rail lines. Good, the powers that be haven't got rid of it. Still there.

When did you put that there? she asked, almost put out. Done without her.

Last night. Came down in the moonlight. The pipe was glinting. I hid in the rocks while a train went by. Didn't really need to hide – I'd already put the pipe in the culvert. I just wanted to. It was a long train.

Good thing your parents didn't catch you.

Or a car driving past. A few did. They didn't skip a beat. Just kept driving. This town is weird anyway. It fits.

We fit.

We don't!

She positioned herself on the rocks as he angled the tube on the rocks, set the rocket inside its base, made a small trail of gunpowder from residue in the bag, and said, Well, I reckon we should do a countdown.

Okay. Ten, nine, eight …

Wait, he said. She pulled her head back and looked hard at him. Gulls squawked and roared overhead. Would *you* like to light the fuse?

No, she said, and looked out to sea at the wheat ships waiting in deep waters for their turn to be guided into port.

Go on.

Why?

Dunno. Just because … 'Rintrah roars & shakes his fire in the burden'd air …'

What's that?

William Blake. *The Marriage of Heaven and Hell.*

Whatever, he said … Seven, six, five, four, three, two … One.

He lit the fuse, the rocket ignited and shot like a flare blazing out over the sea.

Jeez! Fuck, that's bright!! Let's get out of here.

They tripped on the rocks, she grazed her knee, and they ran like small children, without looking, across the rail lines, the road, and to their separate homes, the silver drainpipe perched on the rocks by the sea, a stranded passerine whose entire inheritance of instinct had been spent.

GUILT

He listened for the sea as soon as he stepped out onto the front lawn. In between working out maths equations he had been watching ships coming into the lanes, waiting for pilot craft and tugs to guide them into the harbour. His seat was by a window that looked out over the oval, over the cathedral with its light-holding stone, over the town centre with its one multistoried office block, and out to where the blue of the sky fused with the deeper blue of the sea. It was another sunny day; it was sunny most days. Silver light lifted everything into the classroom and blinded him to the threats and taunts coming from all angles when the teacher's back was turned. He knew he'd be in for it as soon as he left the building, but there wasn't much point dwelling on that. It was fate.

He listened for the sea as a hand pushed him in the back

and he stumbled forwards. As he picked himself up, his ears rang with vertigo and he told himself that it was the sea. The day was calm, so the sound of the sea was subtle, like a great, full emptiness. And gulls. There were always gulls around the town, and especially around the school at lunchtime. Rich pickings, but always the risk of a stone being hurled.

He planned to go to sea as soon as he left school. It was no pie-in-the-sky dream; it was a reality if he could only get his union ticket. Already during school holidays he worked down on the wharf, taking samples off the conveyor belts when the mineral-sands ships were in. The Swedish officers showed him over the ships, even showed him Swedish porn magazines. The days of working your passage are over, they said, with the strict new union rules, but if you can get a ticket we'll take you on board. Over two years he'd got to know the officers on two of the ships pretty well.

He stayed in a crouched position, walking like a chimp. At that level, he'd survive. If he lifted his head above the metaphoric parapets, someone would give him a thick ear. He staggered forwards, swinging his arms – careful not to flail them, just swing them. To show subservience and humiliation only up to a certain point. Over the top of his glasses he could see Kirsten, the Year 12 spunk, pointing and laughing at him. I bet his dick is small, she sniggered. Wanna look? the boys called. I'm in for it now, he thought, but kept loping on, knowing it was unlikely they'd go the distance in public. That one was a change room speciality. He'd already been stripped, beaten and thrown out of the change rooms in front of a class of girls from the year below. He'd managed to fold his hands around his genitals and stagger back in before they could make an appraisal. One of them said, You've got a dirty bum, I've seen it, every time she saw him in the school grounds, even though he was her senior.

The air was laden with salt and a wispy sea breeze was already coming in. By the afternoon it'd be blowing twenty knots, maybe twenty-five. This was a windy town. A sunny and windy town. He staggered forwards, a school shoe crushed the ends of his fingers and he retracted them automatically; it was a bad move.

You wanna make something of it, you poofter-girl-bitch?

He's havin' a go, he's havin' a go.

See how aggressive he was?

He knew he'd be in for a kicking now, somewhere on the walk home. Then the pants might come down and Kirsten wouldn't be far away with her posse of sun-bleached blondes, the stuff of the beach already sticky in their thoughts.

He told no-one. Almost no-one. He told the first officer of the great bulk carrier *Helen*. They'd become friends when the boy introduced the man to his older sister. There'd been a fling or something. The officer went mushy whenever he asked about her. But she'd moved to the city and was working in a movie theatre. The officer had written to her and received a reply, but that was it. Yet he held no grudges, just thought the boy a wonder for having such a sister. She has long legs, your sister, and beautiful dark skin, said the officer. The boy couldn't work out why the officer went on about her skin so much. I am pale, said the officer. He went on about his own skin a lot as well.

I wish I could go to sea now.

Finish your schooling first. And you should train to become an officer. It's better.

The boy mixed very little with the able-bodied seamen who didn't speak much English.

Nah, I just want to leave.

Why?

The town's too small. There are kids at school who beat me up and the teachers won't do anything about it. They're the sports stars, and the popular girls love them.

That's not acceptable, said the officer. I will have some of my crew 'talk' with them (he said it in that meaningful way) if you point them out. Do they come into town?

The boy wanted to say, All the time, hanging out at the leisure centre, drinking piss behind the pub, fingering girls down on the sliver of beach in front of the station, but he kept his mouth shut. Nah, they don't come into town much. And it was left at that.

As the limit of the grassed area was approaching, he knew he had to pull out of his stagger. Year 12s were allowed to sit out the front but couldn't go onto the path. That was a violation of school rules and could mean a suspension. As usual, the boys were herding him to this point of violation – it especially amused them because he never got into trouble in class and was so quiet it was loud. What's more, there was a sports teacher on duty who thought the boy a weakling, and delighted in his sport stars doing a bit of basic training on the boy.

But then he could hear the breeze and the sea and even imagined he could hear the sea eagle that had nested in an old craypot placed on a post down at the point. And that was miles away. All was clear and peaceful. He stood upright and looked around. The boys, Kirsten and her crew, and a bunch of quasi-stars had turned sharply on a new kid. Arrived a couple of days ago.

The kid had drawn attention to himself by having a lamington in his lunchbox. A girlfriend of Kirsten's who'd gone over to suss him out, to see if he had balls, had seen it. What a poof!

They formed a semicircle around him and started the barrage. The sports teacher smiled and whistled and wandered around the end of the administration building, vanishing into the quadrangle area. The captain of the football team suggested they should take it easy, but one of the full forwards smashed the lunchbox to the ground and then wedgied the kid, lifting his underpants from behind so hard the kid was hoisted from the ground.

Wedgie! Wedgie!

He'll have a girl's wee-wee now, Kirsten laughed sarcastically.

The boy had wandered over, nudged his way into the semicircle, and was watching eagerly. A tugboat horn blasted in the background. It was all background now. The sea was no longer present. They could be deep inland for all the boy cared. There was only here and now, the green grass and the wedgied kid crying like a sissy sprawled over the ground. The boy called out, Lamington, Lamington! That's what we'll call him! The crowd turned around, stunned, and stared at the boy.

The school captain thought hard but quickly: an executive decision. Yeah, that's a bloody good name for the new git, Lamington! Lamington! Lamingtonlamingtonlamingtonlamington!

Two weeks later, the *Helen* was in. It had been six months since her last visit.

The first officer said, Well, not many months now until you finish school. We'll be back in another six months, and if you've got your ticket you can work your passage to Europe.

No, said the boy, I won't. I'll stay here. I'm only fit for the land. I would bring bad luck to the ship. The boy knew how superstitious the sailors were, even the officers with all their training and their technology to guide them through and around storms, the mysteries of the deep. The officer laughed and ruffled the young man's hair. For he had grown so much since he'd last seen him. And his voice had finally broken!

Just having a bad day, son! Would you like a magazine to take home and cheer yourself up?

The boy said no, then yes and, taking it, glanced at the cover, thinking how much the woman on the front looked like Kirsten.

Still having trouble at school, asked the officer.

Yeah, said the young man, that never changes, but I'm glad it doesn't. It's better when things stay the same.

FLYING FISH (COUNTERPOINT)

Flat out in the V8; Acca Dacca on the stereo. Loud. Yelling over the music. Pumped. They're on their way to Geraldton to sort the travel arrangements for their Big Trip. The Boys (as they like to be called) will fly to Java, then board a ship in Jakarta and sail up the west coast of Sumatra to Padang. Then they'll head inland, into the jungle, and see what happens. Swigging from a bottle of Jacks, they joke about how out of it they'll get on Sumatran heads and mushrooms. Better than getting them second-hand in Perth. We'll be stoned off our faces and won't even know which country we're in. Fuck yeah, out in the jungle being chased by Sumatran tigers!

Around the islands the waters make shadows work up against the sun. It's all in reverse. The flying fish skim the surface. Sometimes they fly right through you.

At twenty years old, neither of them has been out of Australia, even Western Australia, before. They're hyped. Steady on, Josh says. You'll stack the car before we even get to Gero.

The killing of cats at the rubbish tip. Picasso. Memory forged its links and the flying fish baking on the deck became overwhelming. All the dead they'd made stank in the tropical sun.

Anything would do as targets by the wheat bins, the pickling air getting to them. They fired off round after round.

Exocoetidae. Exocet. Josh's mother was French, though she'd never spoken a word of French to him. Not even as a baby, she said proudly. The only register of her Gallic pride came when Josh's school project on the Falklands War ('Why the Falklands War, Josh?' his teacher had asked) had gained a distinction, the high point of Josh's schooling life. Exocet. French. Named after flying fish.

Perry – real name Jake, but called Perry by a girlfriend who wagged school to watch daytime television: she called Jake 'Perry' because she thought she herself looked like Della – Perry guns the accelerator even harder, and the V8 Commodore hits 200 k's an hour, the bodywork vibrating at maximum stress levels.

As the sails of the fish take lift and the tail zigzags the glinting sea, orange-red at that latitude, at that time of day, the Boys are dazzled, confused. The kill urge is confused. The girls, the radical girls, are standing beside them. Looking out over the railings, the ferry furrowing north. The girls have peace signs on their batik tops. They are on the run, they've confided. A Marxist-Leninist group from Europe. They are German. This is history, Josh has told Perry, who wants to know if they've killed people. Bombed places. Josh won't let him ask. They watch the flying fish, fast, sleek, full of purpose.

Asians are okay in their own countries, says Perry. That's what Dad reckons. We should be fine. Perry and Josh have hung out with white nationalists on visits to Perth. How did that happen? Guns. At the shooting range. Josh and Perry have handed out leaflets but didn't really take much notice of what they said. Though Josh was a reader, is a reader, will always be a reader. But that's what he claims. Who is he telling? Assuring?

Cypselurus. Sleeker. Do they overlap? Cross flight paths? We've been friends forever. Neighbouring farms. Big farms. Eight thousand acres. Mothers lonely, both born elsewhere. Both with accents. Touches of other places. Fathers hating that. Things in common. Hunters. Ride over to each other's places on dirt bikes. Boundary riders. Are you girls lezzos? What? You know, do you do each other? What? Lick each other out? What? What? What?

Once, the Boys were hauled up by the new cop in town, but he was disciplined and transferred. At 200 k's they laugh about it and Josh hurls the empty Jacks bottle out the window, something else at that speed. Beyond the laws of physics. Fuck, man, see that? No! Ha. Funny bastard. I'll roll a spliff – slow down, you mad cunt.

Flying fish are mythical as well. Of course. 'Fish out of water'. It sticks in Josh's craw as he apologises in private to the girl. His girl. A terrorist. Assumed name, false passport, on the run. I am into peace, she says. But I hate the state,

I hate fascists, and I hate racists. Would you kill a racist? he asks. Where is this boat sailing and why? she asks. It is following the flying fish, he says. No, they are accompanying it, she replies. He wonders how Perry is making out. Perry had wanted to sleep with 'Sumatran hookers'. He was getting sidetracked.

This car is a fucking flying fish, yells Perry. He is *pumped* and the car is disintegrating around him. Slow down – fuck ya, Perry. Slow the fuck down.

But why tell us so much about yourselves? You pulling our legs? Spinning a story, making it up and having a joke at our expense. Sorry! You were giving signals. I thought you wanted it. That you were bi or something. I'd do it with a lezzo, no problem. We're here because of the flying fish. We caught the ferry at the same time as you. Out of Jakarta. We arrived, went to a hotel, slept, and got a cab down to the port. You gave us money. Lots of money. But we're not doing it for that, or you. We're just doing it. *You* took us on board that yacht? We heard your words, your anger. Didn't we fuck you senseless while those big crew-mates of yours listened. We had no problem being understood by the driver or anyone in the hotel. You'd think English was the language here. We even tipped the bloke. He seemed fine. And we've not complained about the egg, rice and fish-head meals. We've not pushed anyone around. When in Rome ...

You'd think Perry was a sports star, but he isn't. He played footy but was middling. He was a lousy schoolboy cricketer. But he is a fair shot and loves roo shooting. He isn't averse to wounding, to leaving them hopping around in circles. Actually, he finds it hilarious. 'Hilarious' is a Perry word. A catch-all.

Wanna feel how hard my arm muscles are? See, like rock. That's because I work hard. Perry does as well. We were on the bins making extra dough for this trip. We'll both inherit farms. We'll take wives from outside the district. Maybe from far away. We'll take them back and … domesticate them. It's a family tradition. Nah, I'm joking! Can't you take a joke? You might speak English okay but you sure as hell can't understand it. Nah. But seriously, if you want to come back to Australia … You bitches think you've got us by the short and curlies. You're mouthy, but you don't know what that means, do you?!

Steam erupts from the bonnet and the car rapidly decelerates. Fuck ya, Perry, now you've screwed it. The car careens and Perry rights it onto the gravel shoulder, hitting the brakes, skidding, fishtailing back onto the bitumen and then back onto the shoulder. Pounding the wheel, shrieking, Cunt cunt cunt of a thing! Josh hands him the spliff which he'd arced up just before. Perry grabs it, tokes hard, holds it, then slumps back into the seat. Fucken hell, sorry mate, he says. They are friends to the core.

I don't get all this political shit, says Perry to 'his' girl. I've handed out some pamphlets. Keep everything in its place, I reckon. Yeah, it's nice being next to you. Yes, it's nice. It's so damned humid. I'm sweating like a pig. Probably puts you off.

Okay. We'll have to hitch. Let's just get to Gero and sort the trip out and then worry about the car.

Perry, you've changed. We've only been on this boat for a day and you're saying I've changed? I changed when we got into the Sandman. I changed when we boarded the yacht with the clothes we stood up in. I changed when I begged my girl for more. For more. But then again, you've changed too. You're an ocean of change. I don't know you anymore. Did she ask you again? To do it? Yeah, she did. Will you? Might. And you? Same. Blood brothers.

He's stopping. Grab the bag. I've got the shit down my pants. Okay. Long time since I've seen a Sandman panel van done up like that. See what it had on the side? Repainted. Some kind of beast.

We'll just store the stuff in our bags and carry it, casual-like. If it goes off before we get there, fuck it. Pain in the arse, but we won't know much about it. You know, I like her. I like mine as well. They might like it where we come from? Good place to hide. Yeah! Fuck, did you see that flying fish. Must have flown miles. Nah, it went in then out. Fucked the water. Yeah …

Hey Josh, Perry calls, reaching the PV first. It's a couple of chicks driving. I thought it was a pair of hippie blokes. Josh reaches the car. He is studying the paintwork. That's a flying fish, he says. A what? A flying fish. Looks magic. Yep, going to Gero. You girls just cruising around, on holidays or something? Yep, great, we'll climb in the back. Sound like Germans to me, says Josh to Perry as he turns the handle to open the hatchback. Look strung out. Should we go with them? Yeah, why not. Might get a root! Right. Let's go.

A Sumatran prison would be a bad move, Perry. Yeah, true mate, but to tell the truth, I've got nowhere to go anyway. Not really. And it might not happen. You know. I'm sick of the farm. Of inland. I like the sea. I like the air. I like the tropics. The flying fish. Water and air. You're sounding poetic, Perry. Yeah, mate. It's frightening, ain't it!

They are reported missing at around the same time as the car is towed into town. The engine has been cooked. There is no trace of the Boys. Their passports can't be found but there is no record of them having left the country. The travel agent hasn't seen them. No, not at all. Their mothers insist they were going to see the travel agent, to book their trip.

The fish flew out of the sea and landed on the steel decking of the ferry. What do you reckon they look like inside, girls? he asks as he picks it up, wriggling, placing his fingers under the gills and bending the head back until the neck snaps. Must be a complex organism. Don't be an arse, Perry, can't you see it's upsetting the girls? Upsetting them? Doesn't bother them much to bump off a few *capitalist pigs* in Italy, does it? You're losing it, mate. Come on, girls, leave him. He gets like this. Don't worry, we'll go through with it. You can count on us. We're convinced.

It is the strangeness of it all. That's why they're missed. It doesn't make sense. Everyone knows they were in the car. The car broke down. Then they vanished. No-one saw anything, no-one knows anything. It was the end of the harvest and people were thinking about Christmas and New Year's and spending their wheat cheques. The next working year, the next school year. The dams drying up, winter creeks dried to their bones. Town swimming pools overstocked with slippery children, frazzled adults. Waiting for the heat to subside, the first rains to come, seeding … making hay while the sun shone. Old accents grow a little fainter, the dirt and dust work on the sound of voices. There's no reward out for information. Why would there be? There'll be an explanation.

Something will turn up, or they'll be forgotten and it won't matter, not really.

ARGONAUT

Not a beachcomber. No. Never. Not really. The collection and collation of flotsam and jetsam, the pocketing of shells, the skimming of pebbles, polished by the earth-roll, into the waves. No. Incidental.

Also the torn shirt flapping in the breeze. The gnarled, salt-and-pepper hair on head and chest. The frayed denim shorts.

His shack not far over the dunes, with their drift bringing them closer. Casual work, few hours here and there. Not much required for upkeep. Why bother? No need for electricity. Sun-up sundown. Night day. Diurnal nocturnal.

A young woman had been there. In the shack. On the beach. Surfing, smoking his dope, moving on. That's okay. Come and go, come and go. When she'd been right around the coast, the whole trek, the entire country, she'd drop back in. Older. Maybe she'd stay and inherit. Who else would he leave to? How long ago was that? Two, three months? Years?

You sound like a teacher, she'd said. I was. A teacher. Can you guess what I taught?

Nah, you just sound like a teacher. Teacher of anything. Like you know something that others don't, that you want to tell them but hold back. Until it's time. Until it's due to be taught.

Curriculum?

Yes, that's it.

There's a sea eagle, nests on that old lookout. People don't swim here now. Sharks. Surfers. Rips. But once they tried. Surfers leave it alone for the eagle. You leave it alone.

Yes, Teacher.

Right time, right place. Or wrong.

On the raft of pickets, fencing wire, and forty-four gallon drums, a sheep. A golden merino sheep in its prime. A ram. A mighty beast with curling horns and a bleat that was a bark. Catching the smallest of the set of waves, until until until. The raft crashed into shallower waters and the ram managed to remain on board and upright, the raft holding together in the surf. It didn't cling but stood firm, hooves braced.

The sea ram was close enough to the shore to leap down, though its hooves sank and it struggled in the soft sand. Assist? Watch from a distance? Marvel?

Venture closer. No recoil. Steam out of the nostrils. Snorting, stomping in the froth, fighting hard to keep upright. Horns down, to butt, to ram?

Run back and get an old leg-rope to use as a lead? Lead it

up from the ocean's edge, up through the hills, to the dry land. The paddocks. Sheep lands? Sheep were a fair way inland. Mainly cows in the district, and vast distances between them. Not sheep country. Not the land of the Golden Ram. But out there, goats, and camels, even. And the shooters who hunt them as monsters. Who'd hunt the Golden Ram. What to do?

Ram treads steadily up the shore, arresting its slide, imbalance. It glances back at the raft, struggling in the foam. In and out, back and forth. Secure. Grip, pull, drag, up the beach, hunched back ache. Up up so it doesn't slip back with the tide's searching sweep. Ram seems happy with that. Making oneself useful. The gulls approve and settle on its gunwales. Cuttlefish navigation markers in the sand, glinting with sun setting orange to say weather of a different sort is on the way, and the rest of the world held to account.

She could be anywhere now, surfing big waves or complex waves. Shacked up. But then again, she could be close by, almost back. Done the circuit. The big loop.

You should see the stars out here. More than anywhere else.

Out at sea there are more: in the sky and on the water. And you can find your way if even one shows its eye through clouds.

Old salt. In every port. Won't hang around long, I guess?

I'm older than I look. I have fathered many offspring, but none recently. It wouldn't be right, this kind of life. I've done my time roaming, now it's time to stay put. Is this settling down? Settled. Settlement. The kernel of belonging. Flag up. Claim?

Never alone, really. A special place, a ripping left-hander when it fires. And the beach curves like an altar. I sacrifice myself to its new moon. Its old moon. At night the crabs scuttle out of their burrows in the deeper wet sand. Like burrs in wool, they are part of the sand. Part of the world's covering.

Accepting that it's not satisfactory, no way of life for a proud and mighty golden ram. Why hang around? In the struggle to get home to loved ones, distractions are just ageing. And who is to write it up, record? How much research would be required to chronicle? How to find witnesses, collect their stories? Trapped under the spell. Wolf in sheep's clothing. Welcome to the table. Lambs to the slaughter.

Any idea of what the information, the code of my body, is worth? So much wool. So many folds to carry the extra. Caulk the planks, secure the wiring. A week's fodder and fresh water and the gods will reward. If they no longer tell stories, they still dish out favours. Just no song and dance about it. It all having been killed off. I have learnt that the world is an abattoir. The ocean a cauldron of blood. Our blood. Our shared sacrifice. After rest I will set off. A pleasant if insignificant port of call. No rocks hurled at me, no storms whipped up in anger or frustration. I have left no-one short.

Except for the shooters. They drop by to harass every now and again. Look for surf chicks. But not many come this far out. Mainly young men in vans whom I wave to in passing. It's a secret place. Some have given it a name but I have forgotten. I was a teacher once.

Help me with this. Down to the sea, a foot up (or two), all secure. A push out past the breakers, which are gentle now. Not surf season. Remember me. No return. No looking back. I am not an explorer.

The smell of wet wool. A second sun rising and setting. The sea eagle due back any day. Its partner. To nest. Mating for life. Waiting it out. Fish in talons.

Not a beachcomber. No. Never. Not really. The collection and collation of flotsam and jetsam, the pocketing of shells, the skimming of pebbles, polished by the earth-roll, into the waves. No. Incidental.

BAY

He'd lost his car key in the sand between the car and the great granite boulder that jutted into the sea at low tide; surrounded at high tide. He cursed himself for removing it from the key ring so his new girlfriend could use the house keys. He was going to get another set cut the next morning; his son had the others. It wasn't a big expanse of beach, and he could probably focus the key's 'drop zone' to a straight, thick line, zeroing in on the place he'd been sitting near a rocky ledge, but there was still enough sand to mirror the infinitude of the cosmos. He was in no mood for appreciating the irony of this place being called Little Bay.

Yet it was an exquisite place. It was where he most enjoyed being. If it were possible, he'd live on the beach. It was isolated, and there were rarely more than a handful of people on its brilliant white crescent at any given time. But this was a warm day, and school holidays, and everyone who knew about it, plus tourists who'd found it online, seemed to have turned up. In the time he'd been down there – what, an hour? – how many people could have trampled the key, the solitary key, deeper into the vacuum?

He thought about the rest of his keys as he began slowly and methodically to retrace his steps, from the car back down to the beach. He thought about them being in Ania's over-sized handbag, sloshing around in the bottom with other keys, lipsticks, a compact, used cotton-buds, stale cough lollies. He shuddered under the warm sun as sunblock melted on his nose. He could taste the chemicals in his mouth. Ania wasn't much tidier than his seventeen-year-old son, who'd be waiting for the car, looking out of the window for the car, playing the stereo louder and louder as he got more frustrated. Pissing the neighbours off, for sure. He was a kid with no respect.

Either side of the sandy track sloping down to the beach, a thick screen of vegetation threw shadows across the path. A southerly breeze was picking up, producing a strobe effect of shadow and light on the sand as melaleuca and wattle worked against each other. A red-eared firetail made itself known; his senses were overloading almost to the point of shutdown. He kicked at the sand, which was an annoying greyish colour at this point on the climb. Why am I trying to start over again now? A 'new life' – what a joke! he said out aloud, scaring a couple of young girls traipsing up to the car park, with their parents hand-in-hand a few metres behind. The kids were still wearing ski-diving masks with snorkels dangling at the sides of their heads. Their parents looked painfully happy, leaning against each other, walking a three-legged race with poise and equanimity.

She really *is* too young for me, he suddenly thought. I mean, she's over twenty-five, but I've still got fifteen years on her. Fifteen long bloody years.

And then he thought he saw a silver glimmer. The key catching the sunlight. He fell to his knees and sifted the almost dirty sand. Shit, only a bottle top. Makes you sick, people rubbishing such a beautiful place. Should be some serious punishment for littering a national park. Not just the pat on the wrist they give out, when they even bother at all. He was feeling vindictive. He wasn't usually that way; it wasn't how he saw himself. He continued to crawl on his hands and knees, wanting to bite the ankles of curious passers-by who had been churning up the sand ahead of him.

Pulling himself to his feet, he scanned the bay, as much out of habit as anything else. He was at the point where the beach joined the track, his favourite spot. He loved coming here in the early mornings and looking out at the sun sparking the ocean. In all weathers – even winter, when great breakers lifted from the deep and sucked the sand away, replacing it with another cycle of sand laundered on the most heavy-duty wash. It would be good to have someone sharing the running of the house. She wasn't doing much yet, but she was still settling in, making friends with the boy as he lazed around, slouching. He said, Dad, she's too hot for you!

Where the greyish sand of the track mingled and blurred with the pristine white of the beach. A nexus. A decision had to be made. He needed to be systematic. He'd always been that. Meticulous in his habits.

He shaded his eyes with one hand and surveyed the sand. *I've never noticed how* messy *people make the sand.* He thought of the long jump back in his school days, his delight in raking the pit flat, ironing out the impressions of the previous jumper. The satisfaction. *How indecisive people are on beaches. Back and forth, wandering around, pushing it one way, then the next.*

The sand scratched his toes as he slowly moved forward. He would never delight in bare feet on a sandy beach again. The great granite boulder beckoned. Already, small waves frothed around its sea edge. The light blue shallows with their moody patches of weed were changing. The tide was ever so slowly returning. The dark blue of what quickly became very deep sea was lapping and gurgling forward. The southerly would bring the chop and waves that would help propel conical shells up with the swell, surging onto the beach to glint pointedly in the sun. Sometimes it brought weed, but mostly that was sucked back as it left the clear shallows where King George whiting darted around, camouflaged by light and rippled sand.

He gently parted the sand with his feet, half forming letters and numbers, then rubbing them out. He yelled at a teenage boy, who ran past laughing, to have some respect and stop churning the beach up like a trail-bike. The kid ignored him or said something like Fuck off ... but he couldn't discern, because it merged with the sibilance of the breeze.

As for his ex-wife, she would have been chewing his ear off. Wouldn't she *love* to see him now, desperate for the key. *That's why I left you, loser*, she'd say ... *it's why I married a better man, one with the foresight to own a metal detector!*

Yes, he thought, but what good would that be, locked in the boot with no key to get it out. He laughed, pulling up short with another thought: his supervisor at work … No point keeping your desk so orderly if your work is never done on time. We have deadlines, deadlines, deadlines to meet! It's got to add up, it's got to balance out. The supervisor was full of platitudes like that.

A plastic blow-up beach ball bounced its harlequin course in front of him, and he gave it a hard kick. It bounced down to the beach and into the water, tapping at the shore cocooned in a bed of froth. Hey, mate! someone yelled. That was a prick of a thing to do.

He didn't take any notice. *Key key key.* His father had put a fork through Mother's inflatable li-lo during a vacation at The Bay. Barbecue the bloody sausages, he'd shrieked at her. Stop lounging about on that thing in the damned sun, turning yourself into a beetroot. And I am sick of seeing those stretch marks. That was thirty years ago, and they'd been the *only* people at The Bay. He'd been a sickly child, and the tattoo of an anchor and a mermaid on his father's left bicep terrified him. His father loathed hysteria, so the boy should have known better than to shriek: he'd seen a pod of dolphins and yelled SHARKS! SHARKS! His father had kicked him up the pants and called him a girl. But he admired his old man, who could build a boat or a cabinet or a cupboard better than anyone else. The glue in his workshop stank like cat's piss, a bit like the coastal vegetation of The Bay. There was something dead about it all. Long dead and stinking to high heaven. Invisible fish corpses littering the *beautiful* white sand.

The trick of loving a place, he decided, is being able to leave it. He no longer wanted to live on the beach, at The Bay. It was an epiphany. He was big on non-religious epiphanies. Couldn't abide religion. He'd seen his cousin Lucinda eaten by a sect. They're all sects, he'd said to his auntie, who belonged to a gigantic sect. He didn't need to say God when he saw something as immense as the Southern Ocean stretching out beyond the headland all the way to Antarctica. That ineffable volume of water. That curving expanse all held in like a bucket of water swinging around your head. Swoosh swoosh swoosh. If the rope had snapped, the bucket could have killed someone! His dad never found out.

Hey, mate, you looking for something?

He was about to say, What does it fucking look like? when he saw the key, *his* car key, held out in front of him like a talisman. But it looked dull, not even a glint in the roaring afternoon sun. Just dull and flat and burnished by sand. A teenager held it in one thin-fingered hand. A hand so white it would be bright red after a day in the sun, smarting with protest. He vaguely recognised this teenager from somewhere. Maybe something to do with the ball he'd kicked out to sea, the ball that dribbled back to land. Yes, that teenager *was* there, on the edges … the edge of the continent … maybe he'd spoken to him. A family game of beach ball. All ages mucking around, having fun. Laughing.

He reached out to take the key, half expecting it to be snatched back. Thanks, he said instinctively, then turned back to the track and his car, turning his back on the rock, the water, the blue and the bay. He wondered how far he could drive before he'd have to refuel.

FERRYMAN

It's not often you see a myth turned to a reality, or maybe realise that 'myth' is just a word to help us cope with the weird and grotesque. We don't want the mythological coming too deeply into our living days. And the day the ferryman of the Swan River ferry service became the ferried dead ... well, it was memorable.

It's not a long haul across the river. The ferry departs on the half-hour either side and takes a bare ten minutes to sail from the Barrack Street Jetty to the South Perth Jetty. Visitors use it as the most convenient way of travelling between city hotels and the zoological gardens. The ferry service's history goes way back; this particular incident took place some decades ago. I was a witness, and it has stayed with me for over thirty years.

Back then, there were no women skippering the ferries as there are now. It was still a man's province, at least in terms of employment statistics, payroll records. But on the day the ferryman last crossed the river to deliver his load of human souls for their tour of the gardens of the tormented and imprisoned birds and beasts, the ferryman was a woman, if only for part of the journey.

I was seated a few rows behind the ferryman, as always. If I did not get my familiar seat, I was disturbed and could not function properly. Most of the regulars knew me, and kept the seat for me. After all, I had always crossed the river from my South Perth flat, opposite the zoo, to my job in one of the earliest high-rise towers built along Saint Georges Terrace as a result of the 1960s mining boom in the north-west. I trained as a solicitor, and I was in on the ground floor when the great iron mines started doing their Japanese business. I went up floor by floor until my view of the river I crossed, there and back every day, was glorious and overwhelming.

I love the river now as I did then. I love the pelicans, the occasional dolphin one sees, even the bronze whaler shark I spotted from the ferry one wintry evening – its fin reflecting the ferry's pilot lights. I am sure that's what I saw. And the yachts and gulls and cormorants. Colours changing with the seasons. I felt every scrap of pollution. I used to be a member of the neighbourhood 'Keep the River Clean' group – four times a year we did a clean-up along the banks. There is no such group now, but I still pick up what I can, though my movement is so limited.

I was lucky to be sitting in my regular seat, because I had been working a Saturday, which was unusual, and heading back home after lunch: peak time for daytrippers to the zoo. Many tourists and local families just heading across the river on the ferry – kids, prams, the lot. I have to admit, I slightly pushed a kid across the bench to ensure I got my spot, but he was distracted by his sister, who was eating (and dropping) a slice of chocolate cake. There was a greater injustice taking place there than in the closest-to-the-window realm. Their mother looked exasperated, as if she'd made the promise of a zoo outing she wished she didn't have to keep.

Though a pretty woman, she was haggard and worn down by much more than her kids. I noticed she wore no ring on her finger. It wasn't quite the age of women's liberation in Perth then, and I cocked an eyebrow. And she noticed, because she looked embarrassed, told her kids to behave, and drew them nearer to her, leaving a half-person's space between me and the family, which suited me fine.

I turned to my thriller. I always read thrillers on the ferry. True, there wasn't much reading time during the crossing; mostly I'd be staring at the light play on the murky water, or looking up at the majestic trees in Kings Park to the south-west, or the sombre, brooding aspect of the Darling Scarp to the north. But there was always plenty of waiting time, because I'd board the ferry as soon as it arrived from the far bank and the passengers had departed. Being early Saturday afternoon, my usual crowd weren't there to exchange pleasantries, although we kept those to a minimum. We all, all of us men and even the odd office girl, carried paperbacks like Bibles.

I love the moment the ferry shoves off as much as I sadden when it arrives and manoeuvres into place and the gangplank goes down, ushering one off. I enjoy glancing up to watch the ferryman spin the wheel and take the ferry out from the jetty, looking over his shoulder to ensure all is clear. Then he settles in to small-talk with regulars, chastising children, and complaining to the conductor (yes, they had conductors back then!) about a passenger with the wrong fare.

But that Saturday's skipper was one I'd not seen before, and had none of these habits. He was frightfully old. I felt intimidated by this. It made me feel vulnerable in my suit, in my high office tower, and in my flat, the only almost-high-rise on the eastern bank of the river. I was doing well. Not rich, but very well-off. I drove a Porsche, racing up and down the new freeway as if there were no law to constrain me. I'd paid the odd bribe here and there upon being caught. I was living the life. I part-owned a nightclub I rarely visited, but I liked to let my rich mates know. I did well with the women, and had no intention of getting 'stuck' … But the skipper's sheer age, his shock of white hair and grizzled face, which I hadn't fully registered when boarding, struck me as he swung round to check his wake, catching my eyes with his bloodshot stare. I imagined spittle dribbling from the corners of his mouth.

His death wasn't a possibility; it was inevitable. I was caught in the gaze of a man already dead. The ferry started to veer off course. The ferryman is dead, I called – no, screamed. Some people laughed, and the children next to me huddled closer to their mother.

The ferry was heading down towards the ocean. No-one seemed to notice. This ferry always goes to South Perth, I called. There's never a variation. It takes visitors to the zoo, to see the lions and the polar bears!

Then the ferryman, now crawling along the floor of the ferry, said, Polar bears? Here? In such a hot climate? What are you on about?

I was stunned. The passengers were sitting and chatting, pointing and relaxing, as if nothing were happening. Disaster was imminent. I stepped up to take the wheel of the ferry. The dead ferryman grabbed my ankles, gripped them like steel. He said, And lions? Lions need room, my friend, lions need to roar across Africa, they need space to roam! They will tear a human apart. There are no lions here.

Yes! yes! I called down to him, trying to prise his bony fingers from my ankle, my Italian trousers. Yes! There is a lion, and polar bears, and even rare birds, and orangutans, and a gorilla who smokes cigars and sits in a giant bird cage. A gorilla smoking in a giant birdcage in South Perth? You are dizzy with being so high in your towers. The shaking of the earth, the exploding mountains of the north have unsettled your sanity. You have vertigo!

We are going to crash and sink! I called to everyone.

They looked at me, laughed, then appeared nervous. I don't like that man, called one boy. A large gentleman got off his seat and came over and told me to settle down or he'd ditch me overboard. I frantically pointed to the wizened corpse of the ferryman gibbering out of death at my feet.

The gentleman – the very large and brutish gentleman – ignored me. Shut ya face, mate, or I'll give you a hiding.

Well, at least grab the wheel yourself, I begged. The gentleman looked at me as if I were mad, beneath contempt, and returned to his seat.

I was in tears. I couldn't drag the ferryman off me. I

couldn't reach the wheel. It was just a matter of time before the ferry collided with the supports of the new freeway bridge. We'd die, and so would those in cars racing across above us. I opened my hands to the other passengers and implored them.

Then the woman who had been sitting on the same bench as me, she of the squabbling chocolate-cake children, calmly telling them to sit and be quiet, came over to me and said, It's okay, I'll take it from here.

I had collapsed in a heap by then, my body entwined with the gibbering dead ferryman's. He started to roar, and growl, and make bird sounds. Then he was a boa constrictor squeezing the life out of me; then he howled like a wolf. No-one took any notice of him or me.

The lady without the ring on her finger had the ferry in hand. She brought it about, and within ten minutes we were moored at South Perth. She even put out the gangplank, and told waiting passengers on the jetty to hold off until everyone on board had safely disembarked. Then she went and comforted her children before saying to me, You'd better go home and rest.

But the dead ferryman won't let me go, I pleaded.

Don't look at him, she said.

I fixed my gaze on her. She was really something, even with what having kids had done to her. I forgot about the ferryman. I stepped off the boat behind them and heard a man say to his wife, Makes a visit to the zoo worthwhile, this ferry service. And pointing to his watch he added, Look at that, right on time, will depart on the minute. Pity the rest of the public transport system doesn't run as smoothly!

I could hear the zoo animals and birds calling and crying to and against each other. A cacophony. I heard that every moment in my apartment when I didn't have the television or the hi-fi on. Once, it was a pleasant noise – exotic – but I was growing tired of it. Time to soundproof the apartment. After all, where we live is about the address we put on our official documents, which we share with those we need to impress. Nothing more, nothing less.

BRICK

Her husband worked up at the Midland brickworks, which was a fair commute, but she wouldn't leave the area she'd grown up in. Why would you want to stay, given the horror you've been through down here? he'd say. But she wouldn't budge, and he loved her enough to let it go. Again and again. Sometimes he couldn't help himself. What's more, the river down near her childhood home had become filthy and wasn't a healthy place to swim, let alone teach young ones to swim in. But she'd been doing it since she was eighteen, and she was twenty-five now, and it had set in. Furthermore, she'd done her junior certificate off the river beach and jetty down the road, and it was so etched into her fabric ... gulls, fish, sand, silt, jellyfish marooned and looking like moon craters. When he was angry after a few drinks, he'd say, It's perverse, it's like you must have liked it, really. Then he fell into despair, and she looked damaged and hurt beyond words, and he felt like drowning himself. He was a scum of a human being.

She worked in tandem with another teacher, a friend, who'd also grown up in the area and who'd also done swimming lessons there. He was gay, so her husband wasn't bothered, but he made crude remarks in other ways. Water off a duck's back, her friend said, as she repeated her husband's bigotries. Her friend was always the only one who'd listened, who'd believed.

The final act required of swimming students in order for them to acquire their junior was a dive off the jetty, into the green-brown waters of the river, down to the silty half-world eight feet below to retrieve a house-brick. She used one that her husband had pilfered from the brickworks. That was his contribution, he'd say – along with his whole life being located in a place he couldn't stand, and putting up with her obsessions. Just a small gesture.

When she'd dived for the brick as a child, she'd failed at first, getting confused and lost, swallowing river water and getting a stomach infection. But by the time she went for her certificate, she was as sleek and efficient as a mulloway; she grabbed that brick as if her hands were magnetised to it, the murk blocking her in no way at all.

So when she prepared her own students, with all their doubts and insecurities, their six- and seven- and eight-year-old questions for the world, the ineffable, and the infinite, she still felt a kinship and a sureness that they too would have an epiphany and come through. Her fellow teacher called her gifted, a possessor of second sight, able to swim with a child's eyes and senses but an adult's confidence and knowledge. High praise. He said, In your swimming is your confidence, and nothing can take that away from you.

When it came time for the first efforts at retrieving the brick, she went over all they'd learned about holding breath underwater, duck diving and treading water. All come into play, she'd say to reassure them. They'd developed the skills. The water was deeper off the end of the jetty, but they could climb down the ladder, wade out, the brick would be lowered on a string (her husband had selected the best three-holed brick the company made, very light and easy for even small hands to grip, its glaze shining in the sun like a wondrous sunblock); then they'd duck dive down to haul it up. There is never failure, she'd add, because, look, I can drag it back up any time I want. Which she'd do. Watch out for the barnacles on the pylons, they're nasty. If you cut yourself, let me know and we'll treat them straight away, otherwise they'll get infected. When she said this, her childhood barnacle scars actually smarted.

She and her friend always ensured the jetty was clear of early-morning fishermen (a city council rule during swimming-lesson season), and then collected punctured and tortured blowfish from the decks, hurling them into deep water to sink slowly into the currents of the river as it spoke with the ocean so many miles south.

It was a hot day, even already at eight o'clock, when the last lesson was underway. They'd started at six-thirty, and this was her third class. She had one young boy who she was sure was going to be a great swimmer. A future Olympian, she told his parents, who only wanted him to swim well because he was always playing along the river and really longed to sail his own small yacht.

The boy lowered himself into the water. The shift from warm to cold made his tread-water strokes flurry, and his body shrivel. She sensed that. She knew that. Everything was sucked in. She spoke to him soothingly from above, on the planks, and lowered the brick. Now do everything I've taught you, and see if you can retrieve the brick. It's not as heavy as it seemed when you tried picking it up on the beach. It will practically feel like it's floating to the surface and taking you with it!

The boy dived and was an age coming up. So long, her heart went into her mouth and she thought of diving in. But he surfaced, without the brick, as she knew because of the tension on the string (she always worried about the students entangling themselves, but the tension of the string would tell that also, though she was the first to admit it was an outmoded method and it was nostalgia that led her to keep at it), holding something gleaming out in front of him.

I dug deep in the silt! Look what I found. Then it was gone, slipped from his hand. She called for him to come back, but he was down again trying to find it. And again. It was lost, and she shakily and almost angrily called him in and finished the lesson for the day.

I will search for it later, she said, to ward off the boy from returning and trying again. I will find it and hand it to the police.

When the lessons were finished, she confided in her friend. It was my bangle, lost those years ago when I was forced on the jetty, among the dying blowfish, teeth cutting the air, puffing hard to inflate bodies that had been punctured by fishing knives and would never inflate again. I can hear their gasping, feel their slippery, flexible spines. And I can smell his fish breath and his fish skin and him holding my hands down and the bracelet slipping in. Not even a police diver could find it. My husband said I'd been wearing a bracelet, but it was never found. Just that minuscule hole in evidence, as they said. And in broad daylight? They called me an exhibitionist in the paper, a swinger. I didn't even know what that was.

I will dive down and find it, her friend said. No, no, I want to, I must. And she dived in, a shallow dive, and a few strokes to the spot, and down, combing the bottom of the river, catching her fingers on old hooks and pieces of rusted metal and sharp shells. Up for a breath, then down, dragging the bottom until the murk and her blood mixed, a call to predators. She got lost and swam into a pylon, cutting herself more. She swallowed water and rolled over until the harsh sun filtered through and its barbed rays blinded her.

She's okay, he said to the husband, who had driven down from Midland, called in by the boss who'd said there'd been a 'mishap' with his wife, and he'd better get down there. I pulled her out, she got disorientated.

The husband looked at the bloke – her co-teacher, her friend. In his distress he thought, Well-built. Nice enough. He thanked him.

Later, alone, she told her husband it was time to move inland. Up to the hills maybe, closer to his work. Up to where the river was fed rather than where it ended up, or sat waiting for the ocean to change it. It wasn't a beginning (such a large catchment extending so far into the country), but at least it was further up away from where it gathered.

You want to give up swimming?

No. Never. I must swim. We can live near a swimming pool. I'll still teach. But I must be able to see through to the bottom clearly. I must know what makes water *water*, what light is doing, where things are if they're taken from you, when they drop from the surface world, pretending they're lighter than they really are, wavering on their way to and from the bottom. I want to swim where there are no bricks to bring back up. Where every living thing can be seen in the act.

TOUCH

He liked it during the busy times, especially over the summer when the beachfront surged and convulsed with visitors, and the shops were covered with numbers crossed out and crossed out again, showing there were no lower prices to be had than during the holiday season. The shallows could barely be seen from the grass banks, lost beneath the colourful array of flesh and bathing costumes. Even walking along the paths, because he was afraid of sand and sea, he was bumped and jostled and felt part of it all. He went home to his small room in the asbestos boarding house, bruised with living.

Heinrich was a pure mathematician. He no longer had a university. Once considered the finest mathematical mind of his generation, he had disappointed the university with his 'behaviour'. It was beyond his ability to try another university, and he wore his shame in the form of two changes of baggy tracksuits, in extreme heat and bitter cold alike. He shuffled when he walked, and he frequently smelled enough for people to remark on it. When it wasn't so busy, people were able to make decisions ahead of time, and part the waters to allow him to pass.

Heinrich no longer read anything other than Hardy's 1940 work, *A Mathematician's Apology*. If he was solving problems in his head, he never said so. He did not own a computer, a mobile phone, or any other gadgets. He had an old television that would soon receive only one channel unless he bought a set-top box. Nige, who lived in the next room and drank cheap plonk, said, Heinrich, if you don't get a set-top box, we won't be able to watch the footy or the cricket. Nige didn't have a television, having long ago hocked his and failed to reclaim it. Nige once showed Heinrich some dirty pictures, peeling apart stuck pages, leaving islands of print and genitals pasted on legs and thin air and backdrops. But Heinrich shook and vomited. Nige saved his hard-working magazine, but only just.

Heinrich loved the long summer twilight. He ate a bean dinner from the can, then spent a good while trying to lick around the sharp bits before rinsing it with water and cautiously drinking the soup. He smacked his lips. It was goo-ood! He felt like pissing but decided to hold off because it would get less as he walked anyway.

The beachfront was only two blocks away. Soon the boarding house would be knocked down to make way for holiday mansions, but that played no part in Heinrich's day-to-day life. He ambled along the footpath, smiling at the kids playing on their bikes or bowling cricket balls down driveways towards unseen batsmen. He grinned at the guy watering his garden despite water restrictions. All who lived along these roads were familiar with Heinrich, not knowing who or what he was, but having long ago decided he wasn't really a problem, even when occasionally he made a loud siren-like sound.

He crossed over to the path along the beachfront. It was a southern coastal town, though palms bristled away, and in the heat and with salt and moisture in the air it could have been the tropics. He was inside a picture, a moving picture. He merged with the streaming crowds, still with much to do in the early evening, still extracting all they could from the last light. He shrieked at the seagulls, which shrieked back at him, and the crowds momentarily broke rank and scattered but soon rejoined like mercury when Heinrich moved on.

When Heinrich was eight, his mother had taken him to this very beach at the height of summer and taught him to swim. They stayed in a motel for three weeks and at the end of the three weeks he could swim as well as any kid. He loved the water then. Men whistled at his mother in her two-piece bathers and as he learned to float he bumped against her legs and thought them the Pillars of Hercules. They were at the end of the known world. She had so much time for him, schooling him at home, taking him everywhere. He was to sit his high-school finals in maths when they finished their holiday. She didn't make him study, only swim.

Away from the jetty and the main swim area where flags marked the safe places, the crowd began to thin. He ambled on and on until there were only a few people on the path, and gentle sandhills began. He could just see over the sandhills to the water's edge – the sea was lapping at thin cosine graphs of shells, those fragments left after the day's pillaging and crushing underfoot. Over and over, Heinrich muttered 'radians'.

Just off the path ahead of him, there was a lady. The light was fading fast but he could clearly see her bending over, doing something on the ground. Maybe rolling up her towel or her picnic blanket. She'd been sunning herself in the dunes. He increased his speed until his amble became a walk, and as he swept past her, he touched her bathers, her bottom. He'd never called it anything else. It was the only word that worked. His mother had referred to her own bottom once when she slipped over. Heinrich, don't laugh at me falling on my bottom!

He kept his pace up, then glanced back over his shoulder. The woman was looking in his direction. He turned away, staring down at the path ahead, and kept going towards nothingness. He counted down, then looked back again. She was walking away; she was far away. Just a regular kind of walk, going somewhere but in no hurry.

After his success, Heinrich touched many women's bottoms. Mostly a casual brush with the back of his hands, sometimes in a crowd, occasionally with the tips of his fingers. He never mentioned it to Nige, though Nige did ask him why he had a smile on his dial these days. Once or twice he thought someone exclaimed or yelled at him, but he grew deaf to that, and shrieked at the seagulls, and kept walking, walking and muffling the world with the movement of the ocean. As the season wore on, the crowds vanished and the paths were bare. Women didn't wander off the beach in their bathing suits anymore, though the beach still held a small clutch of warmth and love. He walked past and watched their bottoms bobbing and weaving, or pressing down on towel and sand, but didn't dare to tread onto the sand itself.

It should be said that he never thought of his mother in conjunction with his touching. *Never.* And his dislike of the sea and the sand had nothing to do with his touching his mother's legs while learning to swim. There was no reason for it that he knew of. He just didn't like it. He'd only discovered this when he moved into the town. Staring at the non-infinite number of sand particles, and the measurable volume of the sea, he grew disappointed. Sand and sea disappointed him, and that made him afraid. But they kept him in their grasp. His work had been deeply concerned with paradox.

But the urge to touch did take him down onto the beach one autumn day. A woman in a two-piece suit lying alone on her stomach, drawing in what warmth she could find in the lowering sun. Heinrich broke from the path and angled down over the sand, pausing to examine a cuttlefish bone: its sleek smooth side, its porous 'floating' side. In a short space of time, he thought a lot about it. His thoughts were technical, specific and conclusive. He shuffled on towards the woman, leaving furrows behind him, his sandshoes filling to their brims; he bent down, and squeezed her bottom.

When Heinrich appeared in court, the magistrate ordered a psychiatric assessment. Heinrich listened to the story of his life and learnt about himself. He'd never known. Never really known. The court considered him low-risk, but had to set an example. He was ordered onto a treatment program, and

to take medication. He was to stay away from the beach. A
bond was placed on him and he was placed on the 'register'.
The police knew about his 'predilections'. Eventually he told
the story to Nige, who said, You'll be wanting to borrow my
magazine now. Heinrich told him it wasn't necessary and that
it had nothing to do with anything.

MESMERISED

Unsure if it was prayer or performance, the girl was nonetheless mesmerised. It was 1948, and she had just dashed out of the green cooling waters and up to her towel spread out on the sand. It was afternoon – she and her family had only arrived at the beach shack the previous evening after a long, hot, slow drive from the farm. This was the start of the Christmas holidays, and a special holiday this year, because for the first time ever they were down in time to spend Christmas Eve and Christmas Day itself on the beach! Every year they planned to, but as Mum always said, the best-laid plans ... Every year, harvest went on into the new year, and their Chrissy holidays didn't begin until *after* Christmas. Her older brother Pete, who was really smart and had only one more year to go before he finished high school, said it was a 'misnomer' to call them Chrissy holidays when for this family they actually began long after Christmas. We can call it Chrissy holidays this year, Pete, she and the others insisted, and he agreed ... though she still thought his glasses were an extension of his brain! She – Emmy – was twelve and delighted to be twelve. The moment she paddled into the ocean, the dust and grime of the farm just vanished. She felt good and clean and alive.

The shack was nestled away in the sandhills along with another five shacks built on government land with only a vague sense of permission. Technically, Pete said, they were all squatters. Emmy liked the thought of being squatters – they'd learned about them at school but she wasn't sure there were really any squatters in wheatbelt Western Australia. One year her dad and her uncles had disappeared for a week, only to return and announce that from next year on, they'd all be holidaying together on the coast. Right next to the ocean! Emmy and Peter and their various cousins swimming and mucking around together.

The shacks weren't much – corrugated iron, planks of wood, wheat sacks, lino over sandy floors. Old stoves and makeshift chimneys. Plank beds and tables. And the odd individual touch introduced by mums and daughters to give the shacks 'character'. That character didn't matter much to Emmy, she just wanted the sea – not to get away from the red dirt of the farm, but to round out her picture of the world as she imagined it and wanted it to be. Red and blue and green. It brought clarity to her image of the farm, to the red dirt, to the golden crops, to the wide blue skies. The sea was the missing part of her picture of the world. She always felt a picture should be complete. The full globe of the world. Land and air and sea.

Not far from where Emmy and her family swam, gun emplacements and a munitions dump – leftovers from the war – glowered and squatted and bristled at the ocean. Barbed wire separated the swimmers from the ordnance, and they rarely thought about any of it. The war hadn't been that long ago, so it all seemed logical and necessary and almost incidental to them. If they did think about the high explosives and guns it was with a sense of reassurance – such weapons helped, to their minds, to keep the Japs out of Australia. And they'd grown up *knowing* that everybody else in the world wanted Australia because it was God's Own Country, and that its small population was not enough on its own to keep others out. If they thought at all about what lay across the barbed wire, they thought 'vigilance', but mostly the smell of victory was still in the air, and it made them feel as secure as they did in a good season on the farm. Drought and storms pushed to the back of their minds, they dabbled in the silver waters and ate skippy and garfish they caught at dawn and evening from the jetty that poked out into the sea, just deep enough.

For Emmy, todays and tomorrows were *always* better than yesterdays. But she did treasure one particular at-the-beach day from a couple of years ago – it was the day after New Year and it was hot and stormy, and lightning broke out over the sea. She loved electrical storms, though at home they meant fire if they struck when everything was dry. But here, when they rolled over the sea, nothing could catch alight but her imagination. She told one of her cousins that it was Heaven and Hell meeting and arguing, and her cousin told Emmy's mother and Emmy got into trouble for blaspheming. They weren't really a churchgoing family – only at Easter and an odd Sunday here or there – so she couldn't work out what all the fuss was about; what's more, she thought it was the truth about that storm! Only over the sea can Heaven and Hell meet and the world survive the consequences.

But it was *this* day, *this* afternoon, running up to her towel, running up out of the luscious water dripping and laughing to herself about how good life felt, that she altered. She did not know what had altered, but she felt a shift, and she felt that the land and the sky weren't just extensions of herself, but something connected to all people. She thought of the people in the congregation in the church back home. She thought of the stained glass in the little windows and how they'd always reminded her of a bright, brilliant storm. Red, blue, green … She wished her family went more often. She wished she was going to church that very Christmas Day, although until that precise moment she'd always been delighted that was not what her family did. She reassured herself that all nature was her church. God didn't want people closed in, speaking to the floor, the roof, themselves, to no-one in particular. The shack is a better church than that, she thought. She liked the way light found its way through cracks, the way the sea breeze curled up under the roof. That seemed more in agreement with God as she understood him.

And back at her towel, reaching down to pick it up but catching sight of something, someone in the hills, someone bowing down on a blanket and speaking to the hills, she thought of that God. The outdoors God. Whenever the minister did his *performance*, his song and dance in the pulpit, as Grandpa termed it, Emmy thought it a great performance.

The best part about church. The man she saw in the hills reminded her of this, though he was so different. But was it a performance or prayer? She was mesmerised.

Adding to her intrigue, the man was black. Black people worked on the farm but she was never allowed near them. Nor in town. Keep to your own people, her parents said. And you're a girl, they added, for no reason at all. She asked Peter at the time why they said that, but he just turned his back on her and walked away. She wondered what a black man was doing on the coast. It was a long way from the farm to the coast. She wasn't sure what she was thinking. And he was dressed in a way she'd never seen before. She wondered if he was wearing a dress. Part of the performance, no doubt.

She stood there, towel half in the sand, poised midair. The man in the hills was crouching and muttering or speaking or praying. She was suddenly certain it was praying. It wasn't a performance – the man seemed alone with himself and nature. And God.

Her skin tingled as it dried in the sun and she became aware of that salty, cracking feeling. Her shins and her forearms and her face glowed white outside her bathing suit, and she felt uncomfortable. Was this why Peter had turned away? She was confused and couldn't make sense of what was happening, but couldn't stop watching. The man was a way off but not too far off. He seemed to be facing nothing in particular – not the sea, not inland to the farm. Maybe just a sand dune. He wasn't aware of her presence. She followed the ripples of sand the breeze had cut like mirages into the dunes, up into the strange wet-looking though dry vegetation that clung to the peaks. That's what holds this whole place together, Pete had told her. She liked Peter. She knew Peter thought she was smart, and she liked that a lot. Emmy knew that she loved what this man was speaking to … what he was *praying* to … and she knew that one day she would know its name.

Sensing the man had finished and was about to roll up his blanket and vanish, Emmy quickly turned away so the moment would never be complete or forgotten. She wasn't sure if this was what her mother called a woman's intuition, but she didn't really think it had anything to do with being a boy or a girl. It's to do with the storms. It's now and it's tomorrow, she said to herself.

Without thinking, Emmy looked straight up into the sun and stared until everything lost colour and the world became black and white. Giddy, she ran back to the water and plunged in. Her younger cousins called out, Emmy! Emmy! And Emmy, seeing the world clearly again in its bright array, and looking further out to sea than she ever had before, began to perform for her cousins, hooting and shouting and splashing, sensing them coming up behind her. And the louder she got and the closer they came, the quieter she went inside. One day I will know its name, she thought amid the noise. One day.

MAGAZINE

That section of the beach and all the area behind, which was sprawling sand dunes and scrub, had been closed off from the public for forty years. Now, looking at the mansions nudging the sea, you'd never guess that it had been a munitions storage area – the Magazine. For a decade after they'd cleared it, it was still yielding unexploded shells that seemed to have crept out of their storage bunkers. Not something you think about, wandering the white sandy beaches of the south-west of Australia. But the war went there too, and the old concrete gun emplacements on the hills are only part of the story.

I was a kid during the war, when the ammo dump was a hive of activity with munitions coming in and out, from ships sailing in from factories and out to feed the battle fronts. There was a long wooden jetty that's gone now. The last stumps of pylons went with storms and barnacles not too long ago. They say a marina is going to be built in the vicinity.

Even during the war, with soldiers patrolling, we'd sneak under the barbed wire and venture a few feet into the forbidden zone. That's a common story, especially after the war, when they'd cleared out most of the dangerous stuff. Kids wanted bragging rights. There were rumours of mines bobbing in the waters, but all my mates' fathers who had boats got in close to the shore, chasing the King George whiting. Sometimes I meet with old mates and we talk it over. The daring, the risks. Truth be told, most never ventured far, never went in deep.

But I *did*, and that's why seven years of my life are unaccounted for, and why my wife filed a missing person's report, and remarried because I'd been declared dead and gone.

How did it come to that? My teachers would often observe that I had an overactive imagination. But that's the easy way out. It is true that I'd sit on the beach, reading my 'children's version' (illustrated) of Homer's *Odyssey,* and stare out to the islands and across the barbed wire, thinking I was Odysseus and they were the lands I'd visit. That gods and demigods awaited me there. It was all so *real* to me.

Not being able to cross into the forbidden zone without dire consequences *was* a bugbear from childhood. One of those things that needle your sleep and lead to poor choices in your waking life. Something not quite in focus. An irresolvable paradox: I wanted it to be dangerous, but it was just too dangerous to risk all. To cross over entirely. Thinking about it hurt my head. It's why I didn't go on to study after leaving school. Such thinking wasn't healthy for me. I was happier labouring. That, and the fact my father died and my mother relied on me to help get us all through. I couldn't have afforded university. But even later, much later, when I could have done so under a government scheme, I didn't. Yet I've always read, read and read.

The beach is a short drive from Fremantle, and not far from the industrial strip where I ended up working. I was made a production foreman at the fertiliser plant, and later supervised seasonal workers cleaning up railway wagons caked in superphosphate. It sets like rock. Rock phosphate. Have to take to it with shovels and even sledgehammers. I remember when I started off cleaning wagons, my first season – the medical – the doctor telling me I wasn't a great specimen but at least I had well developed thigh-muscles. I'll leave that to your imagination. Something to brag about down at the hotel after work. And a rough hotel it was. A regular soak for a well-known bikie gang clubhoused in the area. And, of course, I married a barmaid who took to my jokes … and, I guess, my thighs.

I've always loved the Sound and surrounding coastline, even with the factories dumping their shit into the once-teeming-with-life ocean. It still looks blue. Just south, I'd walk across the sandbar at low tide to Penguin Island simply for the sake of it. Just for the *hell* of it! And I love the penguins. I gave one pissed young bloke a good thumping when I saw him tormenting a bird in its burrow. I said to him my only regret was that the penguin had to witness such violence. But don't get me wrong, I am not a violent man. That was a one-off, and I didn't do much damage. Not really. Just hurt whatever little pride he had.

Strange working for the factory. The phosphate coming in from Christmas Island, doing the plant's circuits and coming out sacked or wagoned ready to boost the state's wheat cheque. The aeroplane warning lights on the great central smokestack provided endless hours of joy when I worked nightshift: staring out of the office, fixating. And that acrid stench that leaves the throat and nose and mouth burning got kind of addictive. And the malarky between the blokes. The stories I could tell!

Funny what you remember. What you take to fondly. A pod of dolphins arcing alongside the loading jetty. A chemical spill. Seagulls defying pollution, the odds; never giving up. The ships coming in, drawn by tugs, the pilot boat as steady as a life contract. Never had one of those. No real permanence. Always on short-term contracts, even as foreman. Waiting for the job to end. No way to live, said my wife. No way.

But then suddenly I went over the barbed wire and up into the sandhills, into the Magazine. That was seven years before the fence came down. There were patrols and more people than you'd think in the NO GO area, but nonetheless I was in there seven years, and my shrieks and calls were never heard, and no signs of my presence reported in any way. Later, it wasn't a case of 'that explains those noises' or 'how on earth was that missed?' Nothing. Just a black hole.

I couldn't say with real honesty that I never looked at another woman during the years I was married. Couldn't say that. I mean, when I first met her, she was a 'skimpy', and she was going out with one of the other regulars who worked on the industrial strip. In the refinery. He's the one who told me that if the burn-off pipe ever went out we were all doomed, that the whole place would go up. The pilot light goes out, he said, and BOOOOOM!

So, occasionally, I got drunk and another skimpy took my fancy. Mostly I struck out; I mean, I'm not much to look at. But I can be generous on payday when I'm pissed. And my wife didn't mind the company of the bikers who broke pool cues over those who gave them lip.

To hear the sea, to be so close as to taste it through five feet of stone, down through the narrow ventilators, over the smell and saturation of cordite and powder, but not be able to catch even a glimpse of it, is the most extreme of torments. Year in, year out. Occasionally, during a storm, spray would find its way in, lifted and hurled, dampening and colluding with rainwater lashing the roof. At such times *she*, the keeper of the house in the dunes and my captor, would love me most. The sea, she said, sent her wild. Me too, I said, let me free to see it, swim in it. Watch fish swim the shallows, waders test the foam, skimmers take the surface, pollution's oily film rainbowing a still, fine day. In answer, sometimes, she'd bring me shells, but they were small and often broken, and the sea barely lived in them.

I've no doubt she loved me. And I can say now, with her so far away, with it all so far away, that I loved her in my own way. If I've ever really loved. But I shouldn't say that. As a child I loved mystery, risk, the unknown. I loved that beach because of the forbidden, because of the fence. Over *there*, the sea was rich and the blue reflecting and absorbing at once. The sand tingling. The magazines with their roofs poking up over dunes, the rocket ship in the moon's eye.

Imprisonment? Against my interests, I'll say that's a

complex term. I mean, her voice through the bunker's ventilators, the door opening into the night and my inability to step out at such moments, to execute an escape; her weaving the crystalline guncotton into carpets of explosive brilliance. With her, time stood still. I was immortal, that most impaired and unlucky of states. My beard didn't grow long, my skin didn't suffer from the lack of direct sunlight. Her beauty was the beauty of war. If you can get my meaning, and I am no warmonger.

But the days are long even for the obsessed, the besotted. And a wish fulfilled is quickly a wish to be moved on from. I retraced my childhood steps in the long time granted, I retraced my every movement under and over the fence, my desire to cross. Gradually I thought about where I had been allowed to walk, swim, play. That had been wondrous, too, but I hadn't realised it at the time. I thought of the meatworks up near the rocks and the blood spilling out and the sharks gathering, and the risk there, where no-one much cared about me going. I thought of the rusting wreck exposed at low tide, where I cut myself on toxic protrusions. Of the times I swam out too far and tired out swimming back, and almost drowned. I thought of perving on that woman sunbathing topless in the shallow hills on the 'safe side', where we sheltered from the sand kicked up by a strong sea breeze. She looked like a magazine model you could own by cutting her out and sticking her on your bedroom wall, hiding under your pillow, burying under your bed, listening to the wind lift the sea out of the dark into your empty, lonely head. She knew we watched. That I watched. Sometimes, she leered back with burning night eyes that caught you.

When the authorities began dismantling the Magazine, I waited with bated breath. I could hear them working, pulling it down bunker by bunker. Soon they would reach me. I told her our time was up. Soon, soon I would be free. I would be gone. Our love ended. She said nothing, just looked sad in the paling light.

My bunker, our bunker, was the last standing. I could sense her anxiety, that my going would be her death. She would fade with each piece of ammunition disposed of, with each stone removed. I hugged her hard to me as the door opened and I was welcomed by astonished workers back out into the light. Let me see the ocean, I said! I forgot to say to her, I am sorry you loved me. I am sorry I looked where I shouldn't. I am sorry I heard you. But I forgot and didn't look back and that was an end of it.

No! I don't agree. No crime was committed. Not by her. And not by me. They can't produce evidence. Of course, 'no evidence of harm is not evidence of no harm'. But I know the reality. And there was the war. It is eternal. There are no armistices, no sides. All is war. We don't seem to be able to get beyond it. And there's childhood. And there's the factory. And there's the Sound.

BONFIRE ON THE BEACH

The fog came as a surprise, even to the locals. Even to Syd. One could usually predict it easily enough, but this fog was odd and unsettling to even those on solid ground. For those still out in small boats, it smothered and confused them and had them flashing lights and calling into the soup. Syd's boat was alongside Carnac Island, and he thought of how the first colonial ships had offloaded their human cargo there after hitting a sandbar. He thought about such things a lot of the time. He liked to ruminate on history and facts. He felt that it would be safer sitting close to the island than braving the fog, but he couldn't persuade his old fishing mates to listen, and they moved further out from the rocks and disappeared into the fog like the other craft out there in the Sound.

He wondered why he listened to his mates, who were

novices when it came to boats. But they played bowls together and they were better at that than him, so Syd followed the usual course of things. He told them to keep calling into the murk every ten seconds, then listen. The outboard putted slowly but surely, and they headed south. Syd estimated they'd need to do this for about twenty minutes before swinging in to where the beach should be. He plotted the course in his head: the shape of a set square.

It gives me the shudders, too, he said, but was surprised at how jumpy his burly mates were becoming. They all wore life jackets; he was an experienced sailor.

No need for name-calling, he said, trying to laugh their barbs away. Why were they blaming him? Should have known a fog was likely. That's probably true, but he'd seen no signs, and other boats with experienced skippers had headed out at the same time. Came up out of nowhere. They do that sometimes. Clichés exist for a reason. Yes, it *should* be in his bones after all these years, but it was the first trip of the spring and he'd not been down at the shack for many months. The bones were settling back in. He was finding his sea legs after a break, but it was all there. He'd been sailing and skippering small boats all his life.

Call and response. Yes, we're over here. Calm down, fellas, just one at a time, you'll confuse them. Swearing won't help. And I won't tolerate being spoken to like that on my boat. One boat, one skipper! They wended their way through crossing voices. To make matters worse, it was getting dark. Always trust the compass; nothing else matters. The shore can only be in one direction.

Trying to keep them calm, he remembered a bitter incident. He was a non-drinker. What his bowls mates emphasised as a *tee-totall-er*. They called him a wowser and a prude, half joking, but it was remorseless. Every week for ten years. He went to the bar with them and drank lemonade; he never begrudged them their drinks. Maybe he should have told them why, but he didn't see it as any of their business. And really, it'd have come back on him anyway.

Syd had been a small child but still old enough when his father fell from a boat just like the one they were in. He had been drinking and fishing under the sun in the Sound, not far from Carnac. Syd had lost sight of him, and after calling and calling and drifting, he'd been found by a family from a neighbouring beach shack and taken to shore in shock. Sunburnt and traumatised. The police had dragged his father's body from the ocean and called it death by misadventure. My dad drowned, said Syd when he went back to school. He drowned in the ocean.

Why the motor chose that time to cut out, he didn't know. But it did. The other men were furious and scared and ranting. They roughed Syd up: old men fighting in a sixteen-foot runabout. Let me at the thing, said Syd, as calm as he could be, and I'll sort it out. He did. After a few tugs, it started and went back to its put-put-put. We'll turn for shore soon. The compass never lies.

Why was he fishing with these blokes? He recalled 'the incident'. One of them, or both, had spiked his orange juice not three months ago, and made Syd crash his car without even leaving the bowling green's car park. He'd had no idea what was going on. He'd never felt that way before. Totally disorientated, the car not doing what he asked it to do. Someone spiked your drink, Syd.

Now one of the blokes stood up and lunged for the side, as if he were about to dive in and swim for it, but he slipped on the wet hessian sack containing the shuddering corpses of the few fish they'd caught. Saying you won't stand much more of this, said Syd, won't help you or any of us. Just keep your eyes peeled and your ears tuned. I am turning towards the beach now. We should reach it in fifteen minutes. Yes, it's getting a little rougher, but I always find the bump of small waves on the hull a comforting thing. No, I am not having a go, I am serious. I am enjoying this no more than either of you! Disorientating? True, but look at the compass. It never lies. It takes away the confusion.

Syd silently assured himself that he wasn't enjoying his mates' discomfort. He was certain he wasn't the vengeful sort. It wouldn't have even crossed his mind if they hadn't intimated.

Time dragged on. The men had grown hoarse with shouting, and gasped at the sharp salt air. Fog was seeping through their pores, eyes, noses, mouths. When they gasped, fog poured back out from deep inside their lungs. They vomited it out of their stomachs. They were generating fog.

How much longer? Not much longer. The fog isn't lifting, though. I'll admit, it's almost solid. Can't hear a thing. Other boats have probably made shore by now. I doubt any are lost. Some might be sitting it out. Fishing through the event. The skippies and gardies and whiting and flounder on the sandy bottom are still doing what they do. We could drop a line. No, no, just being lighthearted. Passing the time, taking our minds off the … situation. And punching me in the head won't fix anything. You need me, really you do!

Yes, you're right! It's a light. A brilliant light broken down by the fog. It must be spectacular up close. I'd say a bonfire has been lit on the beach to help guide lost boats back to safety. We haven't been forgotten. Our loved ones are concerned. They forgive us our sins and value the best parts of us. Sorry for blabbering on, I'm as excited as you are. Sanctuary is at hand. We'll follow the light and when we reach the shallows, I'll step out and drag us in. You guys just sit tight and we'll be warming our bones around the bonfire in minutes. We'll know precisely where we are and what's what. The fog won't matter a damn – we can lead each other up the beach by the hand.

LOADING

The bulk carrier was high alongside the jetty. The youth watched the loading gantry move into place by Hold 8, and noted the fact in his logbook. Crew who weren't on duty were hanging around outside the crib house, waiting for their cabs to arrive at the front gate. Security would ring through, the youth would let them know, and they'd be off to the bars and brothels of Perth and Fremantle until the early hours of the morning. Loading of mineral sand had started, and machinery was grinding overhead, wheels turning and conveyor belt taking the land to the sea. There was a breeze, but not enough to stop loading. He checked the anemometer. Within limits. If it got too high, he'd have to send a message to the operators to stop loading. One of the sailors stuck his head through the door and said in Filipino English, How long? Dunno, said the boy. I'll let you know. The sailor saluted him and went back to talking with his mates, all clutching packets of cigarettes and tobacco, hanging out, but forbidden to light up during loading (no matter what was being loaded).

The call came: the taxis had arrived, and the youth signalled. Suddenly he was alone on the jetty. He could see crew on the ship, and in the distance, if he stood outside, an operator above the gantry. The ship's light glowed, and the communications gear over the bridge rotated and bristled. This was a big Swedish ship. All the officers were Swedes who spoke English with more clarity than the youth. But they rarely spoke to him. He was a functionary. He'd noticed how dismissive they were of the Filipino crew, whom he liked. He always liked the crew.

It was a clear night. The lights of Cockburn Sound bent and warped with the shimmering water and the caustic air. Not long ago he'd supervised the loading of a caustic soda ship, and the wind had lifted, and they'd kept loading despite his protestations, and the pipe had broken free of its mounting and spewed alkaline hell into the waters – the same waters his little brother and sister swam in every day when they got home from school, summer or winter. His father was a person of influence along the industrial strip, and the youth had got this occasional night job, one of great responsibility, befitting one who was studying law at university. His quick thinking in having the operator shut down the pumping rig had prevented a disaster. Everyone knew how hard it was to control things down on the jetties, with pressures of time and tide, of business and officers. He was a level-headed young man.

He phoned through that the wind speed was still within limits, though his crib room rocked with the jetty, and everything shook like the interior of a jet in turbulence with baggage compartments threatening to open and drop their holdings on passengers' heads. He sent another signal for the gantry to move to Hold 1. The loading had to be balanced, or the ship could split in two: great responsibility.

When loading of Hold 1 was underway, he noted the breeze had dropped. He relaxed a little, and went back to his torts reading. An officer was suddenly beside him, immaculate in his braid. Can you please ring for an escort to come on board the ship?

The youth didn't bat an eyelid. It was always the way. He knew whom to ring. The best escort service in the town. They specialised in such things. What are you looking for? asked the youth.

Not Asian, the officer laughed sarcastically. Seen enough of them.

The boy recoiled. Officers, bigoted or not, were usually more circumspect than this one. Seeing the boy's distaste, the officer added sharply, Something to remind me of home.

You mean Swedish?

At least Scandinavian.

Okay. A blonde who might look Scandinavian and spoke German was the best the youth could order from the agency's menu. Be here in an hour. Let her through security and I'll come and collect her from here – call through to the ship and ask for Deck Officer H.

The youth himself was a virgin. He always fancied the escorts, whatever the occasion, whoever they were. He wouldn't have been bold enough to get one for himself, and at university he was too anxious around girls to ask them out. It was a quandary. Some of the crew from various ships had tried to set him up after he knocked off work, but he couldn't do it. Not that he hadn't wanted to. He'd even relieved himself over Swedish magazines given to him by crew, swiped from officers, in the crib room toilet on calm-water loading nights, on more than one occasion. He never neglected his duty. In fact, it wouldn't work if he had. He was reliable, precise and mostly honest.

When the girl arrived, he let her through. While the officer was coming down to collect her, the youth spoke to her about how beautiful the Sound was. She said, I hear it's going to get blowy later! She laughed as he started to look worried, and checked the wind speed, and muttered to himself about safety. Not what I meant, sweetie. Though when he clicked, he wasn't really sure what she was referring to, because the girls didn't usually know much about the safety issues of loading ships. He got more tangled and confused, but he didn't say anything further.

Hours later, the wind grew stronger and the loading had to be stopped. He sent the message through. They were on Hold 3. It stayed like that for an hour. The wind dropped a little, but they were still above the safe zone. He got a call from the bridge. It was the officer in charge of loading. We need to restart, said the officer. It's a tight schedule and it's perfectly safe. The ship is sitting low now, it's not at risk. Nor is the jetty. Please give the order to recommence.

Sorry, sir, I can't do that.

You will, young man.

No, sir.

I will speak to your superiors.

Okay, sir.

Start loading.

No, sir.

The youth knew that no such superior would ring. He'd been through this before. Loading wouldn't start if the wind was above the safety. The phone cut abruptly.

The officer in charge of loading was suddenly down from the bridge and in the crib room, in his braid. The youth thought him impressive, and was glad to be told off by such an assertive man.

No, sir, I can't.

Then I will instruct the operator to start again.

But he will only answer to me, sir.

The officer went red, and looked as if he was going to strike out. The youth lost his respect. The officer stormed off.

Ten minutes later, the breeze had dropped further but still not enough. This time the Deck Officer arrived with the escort on his arm. Ring a taxi for the lady, please. The boy did so immediately.

It will be half an hour before one gets here, said the boy.

Then I leave her in your safekeeping, said the officer, and went out back to the ship.

You're causing a lot of stress up there, sweetie, said the girl.

Not meaning to. No choice. It's the law. And a good law.

I've always been suspicious of the law. It's never a certain thing, sweetie.

It is, actually.

The girl began to massage the youth's shoulders. She was *real*, not just an appendage on an officer's arm, or a picture in a magazine, or even a 'do whatever you want' object in the dial-a-fucks of Freo. She was real, and they were real, and their business was all around him, and their lives interconnected. Nothing was separate. One flesh. The amniotic ocean comforting and unknown. He struggled with a desire to log these discoveries, these new facts. But this was his real life, and her real life. Their living lives echoed out into the Sound, went everywhere. The ship hung low in the water, tracking the weather. He could feel her and even smell her scent over the salt, the smell of ships and mineral sands. Her hands were magic. Mystical. Uncertain.

Now, the gentlemen up there have been very generous to me, sweetie, you wouldn't want me to disappoint them, would you?

No. But they're not loading. He looked across at the windspeed and noticed it had fallen within safety limits. As he did this the girl started kissing him, focused on nothing else. For the first time in his life he operated outside his own safety boundaries. In the mild breezes with the phone ringing, the boy held off, held it all in, before taking the plunge and giving the order to recommence loading.

WHALEWORLD

The three children strained so hard to be 'mature' that the adults worried they would forget to have fun rowing the dinghy out to fish in the channel. Not too deep, they said, just out past the sand and green water.

But Mum, said Andy, the eldest child, who had just turned twelve, the big fish are in the deep blue.

Drop anchor at the edge of the green – you can float out a little bit out into the blue from there. I know it's still and the tide's out, but there're strong currents in the channel and I don't want you getting caught and taken out into King George Sound. Listen to me, Andy, I said a short way out into the blue. We are trusting you with the *children*.

Andy appreciated the respect and glowed, but only inside.

As long as these kids don't tangle their fishing lines and lose my tackle.

Mum ruffled his hair as his father had once done. She said to her friend Selina, whose ten-year-old daughter Beth was also going out in the boat, He takes after his father: responsible. Andy wasn't sure if this was a code for something or had a double meaning, but he studied his mother's face.

Beth never said much and Andy didn't take much notice of her, but Sarah, who was eight, thought Beth a goddess, and fussed about her hair and her clothes and the few words that came out of her mouth with exaggerated excitement.

Andy's strong, said Sarah. He could tow a ship behind our ding-ee! Then she pulled herself up – she wasn't going to be excited, she was going to be *mature*!

✑

Andy rowed the small boat a little way out into the blue and dropped the sheet anchor. His heart was in his mouth as the anchor dragged along the bottom, the current taking them further and further out. But then the dinghy stopped dead, and he waved back at his mother and Selina on the shore, sitting down on the sand, returned the gesture. Andy could see from the angle of their heads that they were chatting. Having a 'goss', as his mother would say. But every now and again they looked up, shading their eyes.

Okay, girls, said Andy, when he was comfortable that they weren't being overly watched, Now we'll catch something. He started sorting lines for them. Beth was staring out past him, and he asked, What's wrong?

She pointed over Andy's shoulder, her mouth slack, her eyes horror-struck.

He turned, and as he saw the whale surfacing, and heard Sarah screaming, his first thought was to look to his mother, who with Selina was pointing and waving and maybe screaming as well. He turned back to face the whale and realised they had drifted into the centre of the channel, in the deep blue, and that the whale was as big as a building and opening its mouth. It was grey and scarred, and he could see its eye locked onto him, the boat. He had never heard of Jonah, and he had never read Moby Dick. This was no allegory. The current was driving the boat to the mouth of the whale. And then they crashed inside, and the mouth closed.

Andy had always been fascinated by the ocean. Always. He'd told his mum he could hear the ocean when he was waiting to be born. She'd laughed about it, but Andy hadn't. The problem was they lived inland, deep inland. They only got to the seaside once a year around Christmas time, the long, hot school holidays, and then it would only be for three weeks. That dropped down to a week after Dad died. Mum had befriended Selina, or maybe it was the other way around, but either way, the two families started taking their holidays together. As Andy was rowing the boat out into the Sound he was half thinking that his mother and Selina were talking about moving in together. They were both schoolteachers, and had both lost husbands. Pooling resources, he'd heard

Selina say on the way down, in that kind of disconnected way adults say things, thinking the kids won't get it. But they nearly always do, from the time they can speak sentences and hear sentences as sentences.

Andy had set up one of the farm dams as an ocean. He made waves with a wooden picket, sailed out into the brown murk on a boat made from corrugated iron. He built a jetty, spread shells from his seaside visits around the gravelly clay banks. A few years before, when he was really too young to know better, or to be playing near a dam without an adult around, he'd even let loose some hermit crabs he'd managed to smuggle back. They vanished. He let gambusia and carp and koonacs go in the water. All freshwater creatures, but he imagined them as sea fish and crayfish.

When Beth visited the dam with him once, just before his father died, he pushed her in the sludgy water and told her to be a mermaid. She couldn't swim properly and though the water was shallow at that time of year, her feet stuck in the muddy bottom and he had to wade in and pull her out. He said he was Jesus and could walk on water, which made her more furious. She slapped him and ran, bedraggled, off through the stubble to the house where her mother was drinking shandies on the verandah with his parents.

Humpbacks and southern right whales steamed through the waters. But whale-watching time is between June and October, and much to his regret, Andy and his family were never there at that time. But they'd been to Whaleworld.

Though horrified by the whaling station's history, Andy became addicted, and they had to visit there every time. He pictured battles between whales and great white sharks. He loved sharks.

The whale that took Andy and Beth and Sarah into its mouth was not one of the recognised species known to the area, or indeed anywhere else. But it was the eternal whale, the archetype of the imagination. Inside its mouth, its belly, Andy and Beth would grow old and be forced to share their lives. Sarah would remain ever the same age. They would be Sarah's surrogate parents. Bits of flotsam and jetsam, even other wrecked dinghies, would provide building materials. Whale oil lamps would burn eternally. They would spend years plotting their escape, but in the end accept their fate, their place. Others would be swallowed and join them but wouldn't survive long – the will to live inside the whale would be limited, and they would grow mad and perish. That would be the hardest thing to witness.

When they got back from their holiday, Selina and Andy's mother did move in together. They announced to the children that next year they'd holiday somewhere else. It was time for a change. They understood Andy's disappointment, but it was good to broaden one's horizons. There's so much more to see out in the world. Andy's reply: But oceans cover almost seventy percent of the world. You can't deny them. You can't pretend they're not there. They will rise up and cover us all in the end.

Humouring Andy, and feeling she had his measure, Selina said, Then you'll have all the time in the world to spend with them. Let's do something else in the meantime.

Next Christmas they flew to the Australian Alps, and spent their time hiking. As they flew out of Perth, Andy looked down at the ocean and saw the whale's mouth gaping. He looked deep down into its belly and saw himself and Beth cuddling together against the cold, and Sarah asleep at their feet, salt water lapping about her.

THE UNFINISHED HOUSE

The wind tried to wrap itself around the glowing steel frame but couldn't find purchase. It roared up out of the ocean, but failed to get much more than a shimmer from the unfinished house – a skeleton still waiting for flesh. Nonetheless, a high-pitched whistling, as unsettling as a scream, said that house and wind were battling each other in ways that might not be seen or understood.

Sand and limestone and coastal heath and piss-smelling scrub surrounded it, and its empty eye sockets looked out on the blue-black water of great depth that made the immensity of the southern ocean. Even in the high winds, gulls tried to settle on the frame, their corrosive droppings raising flustered patches on the metal. But after fighting the winds for longer than one would think possible, they'd spread their wings and be lifted out at an acute angle, rising slowly and jaggedly like kites.

The house had been left in this unfinished state for five years.

In order to keep upright, Meredith held on tightly to Li-an's arm. He'd brought her down to look at the ocean, but as her hair whipped her eyes and salt formed a patina over her face, she kept glancing back and examining the house. Something wasn't quite right. Didn't fit. Or fitted *too* well. It didn't add up for her. *Not* just a case of not being finished. That really had nothing to do with it. She couldn't work it out. She felt strangely inarticulate.

Li-an's gaze was fixed determinedly on the ocean, and subtly – not so difficult in the strong wind – he angled his arm and tilted, twisting Meredith's body back towards the ocean, make it more difficult for her to twist and look over her shoulder.

Meredith yelled into the wind, Whose house is that, Li-an?

Li-an didn't react. Words were rushed away and shredded before they left the mouth. Meredith forced her lips into Li-an's ear, which she cupped with her hands. Whose house is that?

Li-an placed his arm protectively around Meredith, as if she were about to be blown and dragged down the granite cliffs into the ocean, which was grinding froth and swirling paint far below them, while just beyond the breakers it was throwing reflections of the sky sharply at the cliffs and up at the shining house frame. She almost fought him, but felt vulnerable enough to give way and be taken from the edge of the continent, back up the narrow wallaby path through the scrub. She didn't try to look at the house again. Vertigo had bent her will.

༄

Hubris, said Li-an.

What? asked Meredith, washing the dishes while Li-an wiped.

It was hubris to try to keep the wind and the spray and the ocean out, he said. It might be a long way up from the ocean, but you get king waves here, reach right up over the top of the cliffs and drag anything there back into the sea. They are unpredictable. They come without warning. You might be looking out onto a calm ocean, with sunlight casting its brilliance and blindness on the surface, and then a huge surge will rise up and suck you down. Crushed in the machine of the ocean. It is merciless.

Meredith had been going out with Li-an for almost six months and had never heard him speak like that. He was a taciturn man, and she liked that. Her ex had been a loud-mouthed, large-featured man, into body-building. He ran the gymnasium in this coastal town which was working hard to become a small city. Bob had been a picker and a mocker, always finding fault with her clothes, her talk, her body. He'd even said to her one day, I love your tits – they hang just right for me – but I think you need to do some heavy-duty work on your arse … I'll work out a program for you, tailored to fit your defects. Really she'd been with him because, coming to the town to teach, she'd been lonely, and joined the gym for some kind of social contact outside work, only to find that most of the new teachers had done the same, and really didn't feel like talking with each other after spending the day a classroom or two apart. He'd picked her up so easily it embarrassed her.

Li-an actually *was* a teacher, but one who'd been in the town for ten years. He'd been married to yet another teacher who'd died some years ago.

He didn't say much. I talk a lot, she'd say, but I am an English teacher. You're a maths teacher, you don't need to talk much. He'd always frown and shake his head, but they both knew she only said it to stir him up. He almost liked that about her. He needed to come back out of his shell.

∽

Li-an, she asked, days later, tell me the story of that unfinished house. I know you know. I am trying to be sensitive, but it's starting to annoy me not knowing.

It's got nothing to do with me, said Li-an. You've got nothing to be sensitive about.

Then why are you so weird about it?

Weird? What do you mean?

Well, weird … just weird. When we were down there I felt you pulling me away. You wouldn't answer my questions. Then there was the hubris soliloquy the other night. Then yesterday, when I asked to visit that spot again, you got shirty.

Shirty?

Annoyed.

No, I didn't.

Why did you take me there in the first place? It's out of the way, I'd never heard of it before. I needn't have gone there. It's not a local talking point. There are more dramatic and accessible tourist spots with lookouts and no steel skeletons to distract the eye!

Don't *you* get so annoyed, Meredith. I don't like it when you're *annoyed*.

She appreciated he wasn't criticising her but was genuinely frustrated by her upset. She wound it down a notch.

Sorry, I wasn't meaning to get under your skin, to turn you inside out, Li-an.

You weren't. You're not. Truth is, I just took you there because it's a spot I really like. It's dangerous, but only sometimes. And I didn't take you to the edge. I love its noise, its lack of calm. And yet it is so lonely and isolated and has its own peace.

You love its contradictions, she said.

Yes. It's almost a paradox.

That works in language and in maths, Li-an?

Nothing to do with either, he laughed, though slightly irritated.

Meredith didn't like it when Li-an got called away on 'family business' in the city, 500 kilometres north-west. He said, That means you must love me now. Separation anxiety.

Either that or I don't trust you! She laughed nervously.

I'll be in constant contact. Keep your phone with you at all times. I'll ring and text and I can use Skype at my mother's.

Meredith had never met Li-an's mother in the flesh, but knew her well via Skype, though Mother, as she liked to be called, always shook her camera around when Meredith got on to say hello, as if that would bring her into focus in some deeper way. Mother, said Meredith, you're just making it hard for me to see you. When you shake the camera like that you blur. Bah, said Mother.

∽

Since that one and only time with Li-an, Meredith hadn't been back to the unfinished house on the cliffs. As soon as Li-an was ensconced at Mother's in the city, she thought she'd take a drive and a walk out on the 'wild coasts' (as the tourist brochures advertised), and have a closer look at the house that had so bothered her.

She wasn't sure why she felt impelled to go in Li-an's absence. Why his leaving brought it to mind so strongly. She'd only ever had an urge this strong when she was giving up smoking.

As she was leaving, the phone rang.

Yes, Li-an, I am fine. Are you behaving? You have spent up big at Wooldridges? Your students will love you. More maths problems for them to solve. Yes, yes, my darling, I do believe maths is a beautiful thing!

She got in the car, turned the phone off, and tossed it on the passenger's seat.

∽

As the wind shook her, she wondered if her body would take it or just rattle apart. Limbs and vessels tangled and torn. Whether it would hold up to the buffeting. She thought of Bob: whether, if she'd stuck to his program, that would have helped her out in the battle to keep her footing. A better arse for better leverage on the surface of an unstable world. The wind seemed to come from all directions at once. Stepping onto the house's pad and into its anatomy, she covered her ears to muffle the pinging and whining of the steel which, to look at, barely seemed to shudder.

She realised how perfectly it was structured. How symmetrical, how mathematical its shape. The house spiralled into the centre. It was like being inside a shell. Because the metal glinted gold in the distance, she'd assumed it was the play of sunlight and glare cast off the ocean far below. But it was in fact painted gold. The gold had flaked and worn through in parts, and bird shit had eaten it away, but it was a golden house in the shape of a spiral. She suddenly thought, Fibonacci! She'd spent many evenings listening to Li-an praise and worship the Fibonacci numbers.

Though she'd arrived early in the afternoon, she suddenly found it was late. Dusk had arrived. Only the loss of the last intense rays of the setting sun snapped her out of her trance. She'd been walking the skeleton, measuring with footsteps, counting. Why it was what it was, where it was, and why it couldn't be finished. An epiphany. A revelation. She wanted to text Li-an and tell him she'd worked out the house. She reached for her phone then realised she'd left it in the car. Had wanted to leave it in the car. She felt bereft. Probably wouldn't get a signal out here anyway, she reassured herself.

And then it was dark. There was no moon. Clouds were rolling in, fast. The wind was confusing, as always. She forced herself to step out off the house pad onto the heath. She could smell the sea. She had to walk slightly down towards it, then turn to find the track. Where had the light gone? And so quickly? Even through the wind she could smell the pissy odour of scrub that indicated the wallaby path was close. She fell to her hands and knees and crawled.

And then she thought, Hubris. Perfection is hubris. And the ocean so immense, so rough. But deep down, down past the gnashing rocks, down to the core of where king waves are formed and yet are barely felt, there was peace. Perfection without hubris. And the wind and the night and the cliffs had her in their grasp. Falling is like a wave with all water sucked out. Gravity and fluids and momentum and inertia. And the ragged edge of the coast, the ragged edge of knowing all people who want company and solitude.

THE BOUQUET

I was heading home after a week away shearing. I'd been caught behind this old Nissan for too long. Double white lines then a clear spot, and the one truck on the damned road appeared and I had to hold back. Would have been a head-on. Then another set of double white lines. It's always when you're tired. I was glad I skipped the cut-out – inevitably I would have made the long drive after putting a few away, though it doesn't make me proud to say so – and as we finished at lunch I could go early. It was a three-hour journey.

The sheds these days are getting further away. The drought means farmers are culling their sheep. Less work. Once, I could almost shear from home, joining up with the team in the morning, heading back at night. And when the working sheds were out my way, the team bus would cruise past and I had nothing to worry about except how many I'd do that day. A few drinks after the last run – no problem. But now it was away for weeks at a time, staying over in quarters on the big properties further out.

That old Nissan was doing forty under the speed limit and really starting to piss me off. I was on its tail, giving it the charge. It wavered, and I expected the driver to slam on the brakes. In the rapidly fading light I could just make out a couple up front – a man driving, a female passenger – and maybe a kid or a dog bobbing about in the back. I dropped off the pace a bit. A kid shouldn't die for the stupidity of their parents. And then something flew out of the front passenger's window and the car accelerated away, at high speed. I was so taken aback I slowed down, stopped, and reversed back to where the thing had landed on the side of the road.

It was a bouquet of flowers. An expensive bunch of red roses. I opened the door, reached out and grabbed it. I counted eleven. I took the bouquet, and placed it on the passenger's seat beside me. It had survived rough treatment remarkably well, as if it had just floated down onto the ground. Even the cellophane around it looked crisp and fresh, held snugly in place by a red ribbon.

I know we all say it too often in life – I don't know what possessed me. But truly, it's the only way of putting it. Some gremlin had got inside me; something out of character happened. I set off in high-speed pursuit of the rose throwers for no particular reason and with no purpose in mind other than to catch the Nissan, to catch and confront the occupants. There were no words inside my head, no action to accompany the confrontation.

You've got to understand that I am a meticulous man. Always have been. As a kid I collected footy cards, and kept a record of every point and goal kicked by every team. I was a 'stats boy', as my grandfather proudly said. And in the shed I know everyone's tally – which leads some to say I'm hungry, but it's not that, it's just an interest. You see, in the movie *Sunday Too Far Away*, when the shearers compete for the honour of being the best, the numbers matter as much as the outcome. That's me.

Unbelievably, the Nissan had found new legs, as if shedding the bouquet's weight gave it extra grunt. I couldn't catch it. It must have been doing thirty *over* the speed limit. But damn it, this was a challenge, and no old Nissan was going to outrun my Commodore V8 sports edition. I planted it. The V8 drank the juice and I flew. I was on the Nissan's tail in seconds. Then the bastard hit the brakes at speed and I almost slammed into the back of him. I pounded the horn and flashed my lights on and off. It was dark out there now.

The Nissan was crawling, and I was crawling behind it. I tried to make out what the occupants were up to. Were they arguing? Having a go at each other? But the adults remained still, and the kid or dog still bobbed around in the back.

I flashed my headlights and hit the horn again, and wound down my window to give a 'move over' sign with my hand, not that they could see it. I then overtook and cut in front of them, trying to force them to stop. Nothing. They just followed slowly behind. I raced ahead and stopped the car right across the lane at an angle, thinking they'd have to stop too, but they just cut around me on the gravel shoulder. In the headlights as they passed I could clearly see a bald man driving and a woman with extraordinarily long hair, and yes, a dog, maybe a retriever, bobbing up and down on the back seat, maybe barking.

I couldn't see the expressions on their faces, it was too quick and the light was all wrong and I was stunned by their tactics. They seemed to be looking ahead, not deviating from their eternally forward vision. Compelled, obsessed, in a trance? And the dog bobbing up and down, barking. That would send me insane. Shut up, ya mutt! I called out, though I could hear nothing other than the throbbing of my V8.

I sat in my car there, angled across the road in a way so dangerous I would have condemned anyone else who pulled such a stunt. I sat and reached for the bouquet, running my hands down the rose stems, pricking myself, sucking the blood from my fingertip. I turned the interior light on and studied the roses' rich colour, richer than the colour of the blood that I was tasting. The nearly opened buds were richly perfumed, and I smelt them deeply. They were perfectly formed.

I thought back to my marriage. I had bought my wife roses for each of our seven anniversaries. Just like this, in just this state. She called them 'sex roses', because after giving them to her I always wanted sex. Straight away, anywhere. In the corridor, outside, in the bedroom, once in this very car. I said roses reminded me of her. Perfect.

I wasn't too far from home now. But I sat there, fingering those roses. The entire road around there, around here, is decorated with rubber doughnuts and figure-eights and fishtails. The boys come out here with their hot cars – their V8s – and do burnouts after the pub. It's the middle of nowhere. But close enough to town and the farms they live on to make it interesting. And sometimes they do the run along here at high speed with their headlights off. Anything to crank up the adrenaline, the risk.

I turned off the headlights, I turned off the engine and turned on the stereo. I don't know what was playing. A CD, I can't remember what. I like all sorts of music. We listen all day long in the shed. Goes in one ear and out the other. It's the rhythm you're after – to help the shearing, to nullify the time. I thought of the boys flying over the crest and slamming into me. It'd be a murder-suicide, but who'd know? And what reason would I have for such an act? None. Those boys are just younger versions of me. And I don't hate myself.

I sat a little longer than I knew I should, then started the car, turned on the lights and started off. Headlights appeared as pinpricks in the rear-vision mirror, growing rapidly larger. They'd be on me in seconds. The window was still open from my manic waving to the Nissan. I grabbed the bouquet, hurled it out of the window onto the road and accelerated away. The lights behind me filled the mirror, then wavered. The car had stopped. Stopped to investigate the bouquet. I hit the accelerator. Soon they'd be pursuing me. I needed as much of a start as I could get.

TARPING THE WHEAT: THE WAGES OF SIN

Looks like bad weather coming in. I want you boys to get down and start tarping the steel-sided open bins.

Come off it, boss, we've just knocked off.

Well, you can do some overtime. No excuses on this one. We could lose the lot if it's not done pronto. I'm going to get the rest of the crew onto it as well.

Including shithead, Sook, from the weighbridge?

Yeah, including the shithead. And don't call him Sook when you're up on the stack: no room for distractions up there. He gets pretty hot under the collar when you call him that.

Might be smart with the figures, boss, but he's a lazy bugger. He won't be much use. Mind you, he does get stirred up. Might get so hot under the collar he'd set fire to the stack. And we wouldn't want that.

Yeah, boys, he is a wanker, but we need him. Get on with him at least until the job's finished. These student weighbridge officers are always the same. Think they're a cut above. But anyway, forget about it ... I'm not trying to stir you up.

Not trying to be incendiary, boss?

Get to it, boys. I'll buy the first round at the pub tonight when the job's done.

❧

They sent Sook to the top in his boots and laughed as his boots filled with grain and he slipped about, sinking and sliding at once. A gust of wind caught the tarp he was securing and almost threw him off, but Sook's filled boots anchored him and he fell on the tarp, squeezing air out through the gaps in the grain.

Get a grip, ya bludger, one of the old fellas yelled. Sook glowered at him, but worked hard to secure the tarp, fighting his boots, which he eventually tore off and threw in an arc over the heads of those below, out onto the asphalt.

Silly bastard's got the idea now.

Yeah, but you know, no boots no work. He's in contra-ven-tion!

Hey, Sook, you're not allowed to take your boots off.

Sook looked at others on neighbouring stacks, tarping against the wind. No boots. It was more dangerous up there with boots than without.

Fuck off! Why don't one of you pricks come up here and help!

❧

You should have had boots on, said the super, dressing the wound on Sook's foot. He'd hit the steel side hard, sliding down the tarp, and cut it. It'll need stitches, mate, you should know that. You'll have to drive into town with one of the boys from the hut.

They're pricks.

Yeah, well, you've got no choice. If you don't, you need not come back to work tomorrow.

It's going to be a hell of a storm. At least my stack was secured properly. Tarps interleaved, snug.

Why do you always put things in such a smart way? That's why the boys ha— find you annoying.

You call me Sook as well, behind my back.

Never have, mate. Watch your lip.

Why don't *you* drive me to the doctor's?

Gotta be on deck, mate – gotta be here if there's a disaster.

By the time Sook and Chook got underway, storm clouds were heavy and nearby. They both looked at the tarped stacks and thought what they thought secretly and securely. Chook looked pissed off at having to drive such a shithead anyway, and had a nasty expression on his face that encompassed everything. If he'd been drunk, he would have given Sook a thumping. It was Chook who cut teeth into his soapbox and chomped at Sook's balls as he lathered his hair in the shower. It was Chook who urinated in Sook's water bottle. It was Chook who threw a dugite, half-alive or half-dead (who's to tell, mate?), in Sook's sleeping bag. It was Chook who dragged Sook from his sleeping bag, yelling, He's having a wank, he's having a wank. Chook had a strong antipathetical interest in Sook. One day Sook had said, What is it with you? Are you infatuated with me? That sent Chook right off the deep end: he'd pulled his army-issue rifle out of the closet and threatened to shoot Sook in the head.

ↄ৹

Blood was soaking through the bandage. It was dripping onto the floor in diffuse, thick blots.

Fuck ya. Don't bleed on my floor.

I'll clean it up. Nothing I can do about it. Feeling a bit woozy, actually.

You're such a loser. You dickhead uni students, same every year. Think you'll go country for a month or two. Makes me spew.

You better slow down. Can hardly see a thing in this rain.

Chook was about to say bugger off, but as hailstones pelted down, lightning forked on the fringes of sight, and the wind threw the ute across the road, he slowed and pulled over beneath some trees. Fuck, this is something.

Reckon the stacks'll hold up … Chook?

Don't call me that. Only my mates call me that – I've warned you before.

Sorry, Chook.

I'm telling you mate, you can fucking get out if you say it again.

Chook Chook Chook Chook Chook.

Chook raised his fist then stopped, looked at Sook's bleeding mess of bandage and foot, and said, Fuck, we're like babies.

Yeah, we are, laughed Sook.

Chook slumped back into his seat, took out his rollies, stuck a paper to his lip, gathered some tobacco, took the paper in his palm, loaded the tobacco, rolled, licked, and stuck the completed cigarette behind his ear. Want one?

Yeah, ta.

Chook rolled another, handed Sook the freshly rolled cigarette, then took the one behind his ear, lit it with his Bic, and did the same for Sook. They rolled their windows down an inch, but the gale threw everything through the letterboxes, so they quickly closed them.

Maybe just one open a fraction. Stop the draught.

Yep.

They smoked as the storm battered the car, unharvested crops broken up like television static around them, and Sook's blood pooled on the rubber mat.

The stack you tarped was pretty good. It'll be fine, said Chook. Not sure about the one I did with Frank and Gazza. We were too busy laughing at you making a clown of yourself.

Yeah, I was being a clown. I wanted to do my best. I wanted to seem like I knew how to do it, but was watching you guys out of one eye so I could get the gist, and my other eye was on what I was supposed to be doing. A juggling trick.

You know that the girls (being *barmaids*) in the pub are gonna make a real fuss over you when you hobble in with your injury? They love blokes with wounds.

Nah, they can't stand me. They think I've got germs from studying medicine.

I told them that. I told 'em you got pox from sticking it in a dead whore.

That's real low, mate.

I'm a . . . what do you call it . . . misogynist. Well, not really. I don't hate women. I just love fucking them. Not talking with them if it's not going to yield a fuck.

Yield a fuck, now there's an expression.

Actually, I love my sisters and my mum. Never said anything out of place to them.

I believe you. Reckon we could try for the doctor's now. It's clearing.

Okay. It's bloody smoky in here!

∽

The tarps held. All of them. Now that Chook was Sook's friend, everybody put up with Sook. Jenny, a barmaid, offered Sook a fuck, and Sook, with Chook goading him on, went upstairs and lost his virginity in a welter of alcohol and perfume. Jenny then supplied every detail to Chook, who shared it with the rest of the blokes on the bin. You're a legend now, Sook. Sook wore his nickname with aplomb. It was a double-edged sword, and not that bad in a place that had Chook, Gazza, Blue, Stretch, Pud and Snake. Those without nicknames were nonentities, soon forgotten with the vagaries of seasonal employment.

Sook's foot, with its six stitches, healed well, and, perched in the weighbridge, he left his boots off without anyone saying much at all. His crutches provided many an evening's entertainment, especially for Chook.

∽

When Chook asked his new best mate to come shooting, they reached a point of no return. Sook didn't like guns, didn't like hunting; he was a vegetarian. Probably it was his vegetarianism that had made things dysfunctional in the hut in the first place. Chook and the others cooked only meat and eggs. They *ate* only meat and eggs.

Nah, sorry, mate, rather not.

Come on!

Nah.

You're not gonna turn into a sulky up-yourself bastard like you used to be?

Nah.

Then come on.

When Sook finally said yes, he knew he'd lost a part of himself forever. He was drowning in wheat.

∽

Okay, boys, let's get these tarped. They say this blow is going to be worse than the last one. Sook, you know what you're doing but for God's sake don't cut your foot again. Chook, you look after the far stack.

Sook's foot was right as rain. Stitches long out. The season had ended for most, but a few of the guys lingered on into the new year for the stray loads still coming in. Plenty had been lost or degraded by the earlier storm, but this was a big receival point for the district. Sook had thought of signing off just before Christmas but Chook had made a song and dance about it and persuaded him to stay on. Sook could do with the money, and he'd become addicted to the pub, the mercy fucks, the guns, the grain. He hated his old self and his new self. There seemed nowhere else he should be.

Though he didn't need to keep an eye on Chook to see how it was done, he couldn't help it. He watched the tarps flapping and Chook anchoring them. Experienced. Chook had his boots off and looked gawky and skinny, almost wizened. He was wearing khaki shorts and shirt. Typical work clobber. Strange, thought Sook, I've never really thought of him as having a body, as being corporeal. Those legs and arms sticking out. Chook wasn't much taller than he was, and certainly no stronger. But he was a brawler, and that was the difference. Chook liked a fight and would scrap at the slightest provocation at the pub with people passing through. He had an odd-shaped jaw and a kinked nose, maybe broken in a pub fight or playing sport at school, and never set properly. His hair was an indeterminate brown colour. Sook laughed out loud at how comical it all was.

The day was hot and muggy. Perfect storm weather. The stacks were almost secured and the wind was rolling over them. Sook thought about the hard yellow grains of different wheat varieties sweating and softening under the plastic tarps. The world's bread waiting to be made.

Was Chook falling? Sook had turned away to secure his last line, but in his peripheral vision he caught something. And a shout? The wind was roaring. Probably nothing. Sook concentrated harder on the task at hand – he did a perfect bowline knot. Chook taught me that, he thought.

Sook had done his time. He had earned his wages of sin.

SNOW

You don't see a lot of snow in wheatbelt Western Australia. This might sound like irony, but I mean what I say. Not much. Not a lot. Rarely. It did snow once not far from Northam when I was a small child. Flurries. I remember people getting frightened, as the crops were green and fresh and vigorous: maybe it's fallout! We won't be able to harvest our crops. And by the time they'd worked it out and decided to enjoy the moment, it had passed.

Until recently, I'd never seen the need to leave home, to travel anywhere outside the great state of Western Australia. It's a massive place. Takes days to drive from one end to the other, from south to north, west to east. I've been up to the borders of South Australia and the Northern Territory, and though it was just a step across, I never bothered, never saw the point. Just to say I had? I am not that insecure.

I inherited the farm. Not a large farm, but easily able to give me a good living. I've never seen the need to marry. If I had, you can bet the place would have been sold long ago, and I would have ended up selling farm machinery in town or down on the edge of the city. And I don't think I would have been father material. My nephews irritate me, though admittedly that could be to do with their mother loathing me. That's because though I am younger, I inherited the farm lock, stock, and barrel. Mum and Dad left her ten thousand – all the cash they had – but I got the farm, the house, the plant. She's always at me for 'compensation', demanding I balance the ledger. That's how she speaks. She married an accountant who still wears short back and sides.

The farm is a legacy. I like to think I look after the soil. I don't over-plough, and am happy to make less money for a year or two and cultivate on a fallow system. I am a bit medieval. I loved history at school. But I left when I was fifteen to work for my dad. He didn't pay me; he said I had to earn what I was going to inherit. That's your payment, he said, in his torn hat and patched greasies. He barely moved his lips when he spoke, but I always understood him. I make a point of rounding my vowels when I speak – I got that from Mum, who taught drama at Northam High. People would say they were a strange pair, but it pained me to hear it. They weren't strange at all.

I was thinking about snow when I decided to travel here. It wasn't a straightforward thought. I was sitting in the green armchair in the lounge, a mallee root burning hotter than hell in the fireplace, when the television reception suddenly dropped out. That was commonplace when I was a child, for the reception to drop out – the television ran on thirty-two volts supplied by our own generator and there was a booster attached to an aerial five times the height of the house. I used to yell out, Mum! Mum! The snow's come on the television! And she'd come in and jiggle with the booster and either bring the picture back into a vague kind of focus, or shut the television down and say, Sorry, it's the climatic conditions or maybe sunspots playing up. She always said this with a dramatic flourish because she was a dramatic woman.

So there was snow on the television and there was the fire, but the clincher was the newspaper. I turned off the telly and picked up the paper, and a few pages in I read an article that said: After a warm and dry winter a cold snap is expected later this week, with ten to fifteen centimetres of snow expected over much of the south of England. It went on to say how sleds and skates hadn't even left the cupboard that winter. Mum had been born in England, right down south where they got little snow, even back in times when it seemed to snow more. She was born on a farm. She used to describe the farm to me, and the soil, which was heavier and more fertile than what we have here. She knew I loved soil. She called me her Child of the Soil. Sometimes I dreamed of the dark soil on her childhood farm, but I'd never wanted to go there. Not at all. Mum had encouraged me to keep a passport, though I told her I'd never use it. She'd say, Just in case you change your mind.

So I went to bed with snow and static and my mother and soil in my head. I fell to sleep half forming and losing thoughts. I didn't dream snow but I tried to dream snow.

I woke knowing I was going somewhere and it wasn't in Western Australia.

There was a ticket on the following night's flight via Singapore. I grabbed it. I packed quickly and drove myself to the airport. Actually, I was no stranger to the airport. Neighbours and friends in town were always asking me to drive them down so they wouldn't have to put their cars in the long-term car park. I said to them, I don't mind, but I would want my own car there when I arrived home.

When we were a few hours out of Heathrow, the voice over the speakers said our landing would be delayed due to bad weather. The snow had started. Not heavy, but making things slow and awkward. I was in the middle of the plane, and I felt there was no reality outside the asylum I'd committed myself to. Give me my own car and a long drive out into the desert. It provides you with all the intimacy and alienation you need at once. The plane was just compression and breathlessness.

I thought I'd make my way north into the snowier parts. I had nothing booked, but it wasn't what they call holiday season, so I didn't envisage problems finding a room. But the snow had set in hard and I had to settle on an airport hotel because transport wasn't working. Not even the Underground. It was like being in a disaster movie. I was lucky to get a room and I could only book it for one night. But after I'd checked in, I stood in the car park and let the snow cover my sickness. My jet lag. I felt out of my body. I felt like I'd been on the tractor for weeks at a time, feeling every jolt, every clod of earth. I went inside, ate something nondescript in the hotel restaurant, showered and shaved (which I forgot to do before dinner – I live on my own), and then fell into a deep sleep. I woke at nine, and check-out was at eleven.

I pulled back the curtains and it was a clear blue sky, but there was snow over the ground. Everywhere. I dressed and went straight down to the front of the hotel where kids were rolling snowmen. I joined them. The odd plane straggled down from the sky, but it was eerily quiet. The snow was quite thick. The kids laughed and I laughed. Their parents were nowhere to be seen in the concrete and steel and glass and snow. We threw snowballs at each other. Just like boondies on the farm when I was a child – though the impact was less (my sister would have cried with snow, never mind boondies). I was a master of snow. I knew all its tricks instinctively. I was inside the television set.

The day was warming rapidly and the snow was becoming slushy. I had checked out and stored my baggage. I ate a meal in the restaurant and went out and played in the snow. The snowmen were losing their features. The snow is very short, I said, and people looked at me. But I knew what I said made sense. I went into the lobby and asked them to see if there was a spare seat on a Qantas flight back to Perth that evening. They were very accommodating. I managed to adjust my ticket with only a little extra cost, though to tell the truth, if it'd been five times as much I would have paid. But I didn't let on about that.

My car was waiting for me in long-term parking. I drove back to the farm with the air-conditioning on full. It's a good air-conditioner. It can turn summer to winter, and I will always have a head full of snow.

THE BET

They were half-friends. Occasionally played together, tolerated each other when forced to sit together, but had never gone round to each other's homes after school.

On the day of the inter-school swimming carnival, they both had summer colds and 'wagging it' slips from their mothers. It was a small school and they were the only two to stay behind, watched over by the headmaster himself; he had better things to do so he set them doing art all day. They had a classroom to themselves.

The swimming carnival wasn't far away. The boys could hear the crowd yelling and shrieking and carrying on. Three schools from neighbouring districts were competing. The school champion, a classmate of theirs, mocked them just before the school marched off in its files according to factions:

You don't look too sick, you two sissy bludgers. His body rippled with pride and self-love. The two stay-behinds looked at each other and smirked. Another thing in common.

Des was the bigger of the two, and slightly lorded it over Garry, the elder by two months. Garry was a nervous sort, but that was more of a ploy, like the snail retreating into its shell at times of threat, but probably quite happy and secure in its own fluids and ecology. If threatened, Garry had a litany of interest-piques up his sleeve, like: I flicked Gabrielle's dress up with my ruler and saw what colour knickers she's wearing. And if the reply came, So what, everyone's seen Gabrielle's knickers, he'd retort: But she doesn't call them knickers, I've heard her say 'panties', and everyone knows that means she's a slut.

Des and Garry did art. They drew rank cartoons of their teachers having sex with sheep and goats. The headmaster was turned into a goat, having sex with a sheep, which might well have been their teacher, Miss Morris. And they drew Nev, the school champion, swimming with a flagpole up his arse, the flag flailing in the water. It had to be said, they both had talent and possibly a future as cartoonists for the state newspaper.

It was a stinking hot day. Garry mused that even with factor 30 sunblock, all the kids would be cooking. Chlorine and that chemical that changes the colour of the water when kids piss, and those lemon-scented gums they've got planted in strategic places so the limbs fall and kill the kids stone dead. You can smell those trees when it gets this hot. I can smell them from here, said Garry. Nah, said Des, that's the gum trees around the school you can smell. Garry looked at him, bemused, not knowing how to tell him that he was making a joke; but he sniffed hard, and *could* smell the lemon-scented gums through the school gums and over all that distance.

The day wore on. The carnival kids would either go home straight from the pool, or line up out front for the buses back to school. Visiting teams would be collected by their buses outside the pool. Garry and Des talked this over, ate their lunches early because the headmaster was nowhere to be seen (they didn't bother hiding their cartoons), and out of boredom resorted to bragging.

Des bet Garry that he could shoot ten pieces of paper into the rubbish bin from where he was sitting. Garry bet he couldn't. What'll you bet? asked Des. I just bet you can't, said Garry. Des shot the ten pieces into the bin.

Garry told Des he'd taken Miss Morris's birth control pills from her bag, and fed one of them to the guinea pigs in the science lab. Des, not knowing what the pills were, bet him he hadn't. What'll you bet? asked Garry. Nothing, said Des, it's not worth anything.

This went on for a while until they got bored all over again. As the afternoon wore on, they went repeatedly to the toilet, sprayed water from the fountains over each other, packed up their cartoons, planning to plant them on the school champ the next day, had an arm wrestle which Garry lost and Des crowed over, and farted so loud that the room resonated and Des punched Garry repeatedly in the arm for 'letting off', though he'd done the most, the loudest and the smelliest.

They discussed shooting through, but as they were about to go, the goat of a headmaster poked his head into the classroom and asked if all was well, boys, using the time constructively, I hope. And if their hearts faltered at the thought that he might ask to see their work, they underestimated his supreme indifference; he vanished as fast as he appeared.

Des said, I bet you can't shoot ten pieces of paper into the bin from here. Garry, thoroughly tired of Des now, and hoping to never have to talk with him again after that day, looked at him carefully, screwed his eyebrows, eyes flickering, and said, You're on. What odds will you give me?

Des said, as per their earlier games, I won't bet you anything … it's just a dare.

Nah, said Garry, let's bet proper. You name your odds.

Des thought of whacking Garry, but laughed. Garry was a dope. Slow or somethin'. Odd. Peculiar. A weed. A joke. He'd pants him. He wasn't sure what was meant by 'odds', so he replied, If you lose I'll pants ya in front of Gabrielle.

And if I win? asked Garry.

You won't. You can't get ten pieces of paper in the bin from here. They won't even go that far. Even I couldn't do it, never mind a dope like you.

I bet you five hundred dollars. So you give me five hundred if I win, and you can pants me if I don't.

Sure!

We'll write it down and sign it.

What? Why? Well, why not.

Garry wrote it up and they both signed it. Des joked, It should be signed in blood! He looked at Garry, trying to intimidate, but Garry said, Sure, why not. Thumbprints of our blood. We'll prick ourselves with compasses. And they did, thumbprinting next to their signatures,

Garry scrunched the paper as hard as he could and shot ten out of ten. He was good at it, having whiled hours away in his room doing the same thing. When his dad was on the piss, he had to keep out of the way if stuck indoors, this was as good a sport as any.

That's five hundred bucks, please, mate, said Garry, who had filed away the betting slip in his back pocket without Des registering.

Piss off! said Des, and pummelled Garry's arm so hard that Garry whimpered and leapt out of the room as the school siren rang, echoing through the emptiness of the classroom, the school.

∽

Though Gary's father was a violent man, he strangely doted on his son as a chip off the old block. But Garry detested his father, and carried out secret errands for his mother to undermine his dad's authority. He poured booze down the sink; he snuck out to the shop to buy food not cigarettes.

Riffling through his son's pockets for a fifty-cent piece (pocket money his mum gave from housekeeping) to make up the price of a bottle of sherry, Garry's dad came across the betting slip.

What's this, boy?

Nothing, just a joke, Dad ... a *pretend* bet I won at school ... shooting bits of paper into a bin ... you know, just muckin' round with a mate. The father looked cockeyed at the boy, thirsty and shaking already. He was in no mood. Five hundred dollars and signed in blood. That's a legal document.

No, said Garry, we're under-age. Garry knew about such things; Des would have been well-advised to look deeper into what made Garry tick. He was no dope.

We'll see about that, said his father. Des Bailey. I know his old man.

Don't do anything, Dad! It was just a joke. Garry shuddered. Every pummelling of his arm ricocheted through his body, and he found it difficult to play dumb any longer. But he did. Don't embarrass me, Dad! Which was a red rag to a bull, and, what's more, impossible, given Garry's humiliations at the hands of his father were legion, and he was pretty well immune.

✑

Des wasn't at school for a week. When he turned up, he avoided Garry. He was a changed boy. Quiet, deferring to any challenger, diligent, polite. When Garry came near, he cowered, looking down at him with large eyes. Why do you keep following me, Garry?

What does your dad do for a crust? asked Garry.

Des's eyes grew even wider. Saucers. Windmills. None of your business, he snapped, finding a bit of his old bluster.

Lives off your mum, like my dad, said Garry.

Des mumbled something like, Maybe.

I learnt from my mum. How to get through. You've got to do the same. Watch out, take the opportunities, keep your head down. If not, you'll get picked on every time. My old man is full of shit. Mum says, what goes around comes around. Your old man will get one up on him next week when Dad's hanging for a drink and needs a mate.

Des stared, half computing.

Strange we haven't got to know each other better. Our dads are in each other's pockets. It's not a big town. I tell you, Des, I bet we're both shot of the place as soon as we're old enough to leave. And no forwarding address, not even for our mums, who'll always tell their old men when the pressure's on. Really on.

It was stinker of a day. Soon the long Christmas holidays. The odour of gum resin was enough to make you throw up.

Des said, Meet you down the pool when it opens after Christmas?

Sure, why not, said Garry. We can compare gifts.

THE TALE OF FERGUSON'S FOLLY

Since he was a small kid he'd dreamt of the ocean but rarely ever saw it. Whenever he could he'd book vacations down south by the sea, but something always intervened, and he'd end up only spending a couple of days every few years by the grinding waves of the Southern Ocean. He loved the way the ocean smashed away at the granite and made white foam of black rocks.

He loved all water. The sea was perfect, but a good river would do at a pinch. It was just so damn dry out where he lived and farmed. He had dug huge dams, which caught water from thousands of acres, but there was so little rain they rarely got even half-filled. But the Year of the Downpours had them brimming, and it was then he made the life decision that would evermore be known throughout the district as Ferguson's Folly.

The Folly was a houseboat, and it had to come up from the coast on a big rig. Ferguson had actually called it Fiona, after an old high-school flame (she burnt him and his best mate), which seemed halfway to Folly anyway. It was a bloody big houseboat and, being on pontoons, would float on even a few feet of water. Ferguson knew his blissfully full dams would drop to a puddle, so he wanted to ensure that even in drier times his boat would float. *His* houseboat.

He settled it onto the biggest of his dams, and took up residence. He read Patrick O'Brian novels between chores. It was a lush harvest after all the rain, and everything was bumper and overflowing. His seas of wheat had becomes seas of money. He even thought of taking on crew. It'd been a long time since he'd lived with a woman. But he let the thought drift.

Some in town wanted to use whatever laws were available to make it a tourist attraction, but there weren't any relevant laws, and Ferguson wasn't about to let anyone onto his place to leer at him. Already he was having to cope with too frequent visits from neighbours and old friends who suddenly remembered he existed. He wouldn't let them on board. One or two pissed shearers had tried swimming on, and as the water level dropped with what was turning out to be a deadly summer, one of his neighbours' dogs made the swim and dragged itself muddy onto the deck, to draw its owner wading through the sludge to retrieve it. It's said Ferguson took a few pot shots at motorised gliders that flew too close, though this is unlikely, because if Ferguson had wanted to hit something he would have hit it.

The water in the dam stayed relatively high given the rate

of evaporation that summer, and his sea survived the climate. Autumn rains came early, and there'd be one or two summer storms to halt the drop temporarily. Really, he was sitting pretty. He loved the gentle slapping of the water on the pontoons when the wind picked up, carving over the ochre clay dam walls and creating cross-breezes that really made one feel as if the ocean were beneath the decks. He slept well.

An extreme winter storm was a delight. One night, buffeted by waves, brown-green waves of sediment and sheep-manured water, the wind ripping fittings from the roof deck, he thought he was going to sink. And with the water slightly less than two fathoms in the middle when the dam was brimming, at the centre where he had the boat moored most of the time, sinking would mean something. The storm threw up Sargasso over the decks. Hay and shit and God knows what else. The inland spirit of an ancient long-gone ocean. It was almost haunting.

And though the dam was big enough for Ferguson to break loose and sail around the edges, to travel the four corners, which he occasionally did – the sheep, down for a drink, would watch intently, baaing and throwing looks at each other with knowledge and wisdom – he preferred to remain out to sea, travelling to and from the shore in a rubber dinghy when need be. As he was a large man, the dinghy almost folded in on itself, often taking on silty water when the wind was up. As he paddled with his single plastic oar in increasing urgency, his matted hair and unkempt beard combined to create a spectacle that would have seemed disturbed, if not frightening, to a stranger; never mind the fact that his destination was a houseboat on a farm dam.

This was in the days before mobile telephones, but Ferguson, being a CB radio obsessive, kept in touch with the local chatter without having to leave his property. He had run a powerline out to the boat from the generator shed he'd set up near the dam, and there was a phone in the house if he ever needed to speak to the distant outside world. But mostly he stayed disconnected, and ran his wheat and sheep farm from the boat.

Ferguson had been married, but his wife divorced him after their toddler's death. It wasn't Ferguson's fault, and the little house dam had been almost dry, but the boy wandered in and got stuck in the mud. Like animals going to the muddiest parts when the summer has gone and the rains haven't come, sinking further and further down as they try to suck a drink out of the sludge, so the small boy had tired himself by working to get out. You could tell that. The coroner said all this in his report. Ferguson rarely went near that dam, which was too small anyway to think of as a sea. Too small for his boat.

People never made the connection when they called his boat *Ferguson's Folly*. They seemed not even to think it. It was just a line never drawn. Other than one person; she didn't call it his Folly, but his tragedy. His ex-wife, Hester, had never stopped loving him, but she just couldn't be with him. Not there, on the farm. She'd even asked him to sell up and move to his beloved coast, away from it all, and start again, but he wouldn't. We can holiday, he said, but the farm is tidal in a way that's impossible to resist. He sounded ridiculous saying this, and as he murmured something about undertow, he dropped his eyes with embarrassment. It would have been *his*, all of this, as I inherited it from my father. And she left, angry and sad for him, tormented by their not having kept an eye on the boy. He'd never wandered down to the dam before. And how did he move so fast from the scrap of house lawn she'd watered religiously with red water pumped up from the very same dam? He was there playing on the sweet green grass; then he was gone.

Ferguson stopped bothering to visit the coast. He never did so again. Two summers later and drought had set in so severely that there was barely a puddle in the dams for years. He did not abandon his houseboat. He built a stone causeway across the sludge – the wretched stygian sludge, the murderous nothingness of mud: neither water nor earth – then the dust that followed. He waited it out. The oceans will rise, he said, they will rise and swallow us all. The flood is coming.

MISNOMER

I told her it was a powderbark and *not* a sammy, he said bitterly. I told her I told her I told her!

I tried to calm him with a hand on the shoulder but he shrugged it off. I noticed a tear in the eye of this rough man who was always proud to be in a blue singlet in summer and a red-checked shirt in winter. I mention this not gratuitously, not as a class awkwardness on my part, but because his wife always told me this by way of reassurance. I made no judgement, and make none, I think.

She insisted it was a sammy, even when I showed her in a book. Even when her friends, including one of her science teacher mates from school, told her. A powderbark wandoo. Similar colour, different canopy. They look different. They are different species!

He kept lamenting, and I let him. Strange, that a man of so few words could get so hooked on them now. Survival. Words had been her thing. An English teacher married to a shearer. Not that strange out in the country, I guess. And he had a point – I mean, a point about naming things properly.

He went back to the beginning, talking rapidly, which in itself was a sign of how hard he was finding it to cope – he usually spoke in a steady drawl.

The problem was that there was a great sammy a few k's further down the road. One we both agreed was called Sammy, and was a salmon gum. Not many left around here – cleared away for cropping back in the twenties. But you still get that edgy stuff where wandoo woodland meets stands of salmon gum, the land changing and not able to make up its mind. And that powderbark on one corner was massive for a powderbark – I suppose you could be forgiven for mistaking it. But I always called it the Powderbark, and she called it Sammy, even though the next big tree a few k's on was called Sammy as well. I ragged her over that. She had such a way with words but when she was stuck on a point, she lost imagination. She could be bloody-minded, you know.

I wanted to ask why, when writing down directions, he'd not taken her idiosyncrasies, her terms and geography, into consideration. He'd left before she got up and hadn't wanted to wake her. He'd forgotten to mention it the night before. Of course, discussing it would have sorted the potential problem there and then. The note he left on the fridge's whiteboard didn't say 'the *real* Sammy', or some other indicator or joke to show he actually meant the *mutually agreed upon salmon gum, not the earlier tree we argue over*. He simply said, Turn left at the sammy, drive three k's and you'll find me waiting by a farm gate. She was picking him up after a cut-out, a drinking binge to mark the end of a shed. They'd shorn five thousand sheep at that shed and the farmer had put on three cartons. He hadn't wanted to drive that day, and the rest of the team were heading off in the bus in the opposite direction. Made sense. But she'd turned early, at the Powderbark, and driven on and on, thinking, probably, that he'd got the distance wrong; all the time, probably, scanning the side of the road for her husband.

And why did she drive so far? he pleaded, his great gnarled hands already twisting with arthritis from so many years of holding sheep and the hot vibrating handpiece. It looked like he was flailing in deep water, an ungainly fish that had suddenly discovered it has no right to swim, that it was all a trick up to this point. He was an alien in his own territory, his own world, his entire universe. He had nowhere else to go.

She ... he said. A pause. I was never good with words, especially writing them down, he said. I should have drawn a mud map. I'm good with maps. I could have drawn the bloody trees and made her laugh. I am *spatial*. That's what she said. She'd laugh and say, You're a spatial bloke. Blokes are spatial. But she'd laugh in a way that said she didn't really believe this. I liked that. Sarcasm is a healthy thing, I reckon. Drains the shit out of everything. It's like the design of shearing sheds. Clever letting sheep and shearers walk the boards and yet the sheep shit and piss fall through to the world beneath.

The underworld, I said, then caught myself as he looked

at me, hurt. Maybe I could get away with it, being her best friend, also being a teacher. Another person of words.

We were going down to Perth tomorrow night for a big feed and a movie, he said, now collapsed into a chair, running a dark finger round the rim of the china cup. He stared into the cup and read his tea leaves. I never use tea bags. I felt glib. Emotion was harder for me than him. I missed her too but my missing her had no place. This wasn't about mutual commiseration.

But I had to come up with something or we could have both crashed through the floor, through the underworld of sheep shit, through to the core of the planet, to become molten with the weight of being left alive and picking up the pieces. My metaphors were mixing so much I coughed, and he looked at me and I thought him beautiful. A moment out of DH Lawrence. I had to be careful. Things were getting in the way. But they always had. There'd never be anybody I could tell. I hadn't mentioned it to her – you just can't – and he was beyond me now. No chance, no chance at all. I said, Which movie?

Sorry? he said.

Which movie were you going to see?

He fixed me with his burning green eyes. It was as if he suddenly 'got' me, but cast it down to that centre of the earth I so feared. And there it would stay. He said, so clinically, It doesn't matter which movie.

His wife and I had worked together on the local newspaper. Occasional amateur reporters. And now I had to write up her death. Killed in a car accident. Driving at night along Refuge Road, she hit a large pothole formed by recent heavy rain, veered off into the culvert and rolled her car. 'Died instantly.'

That was the draft. I couldn't write it that way. It would sound less like an accident, more like her own doing. She must have been driving at a fair speed to have done that. But panic had set in – maybe she'd realised her mistake and was rushing back to the main road, to move on to the mutually-agreed-upon sammy, the True Sammy. But she never believed it was, I am sure. I *am* sure. She loved him, no doubt. She said to me, I miss him every minute I am not with him. She worried about his drinking. She didn't like cut-outs. It always upset him, she said, when the young blokes made remarks about me – you know I've taught many of them over the years. School-teacher fantasy stuff. She wasn't flattering herself. She was a beauty. Hot! they'd say. A handsome couple.

I wanted to write another article – maybe for an issue in six months' time. No connection. About trees and their names. About telling salmon gums and powderbark wandoos apart. You find both in the district. But the uptight ex-city editor on his 'tree change' adventure would never take it; he'd only say, What kind of fool can't tell them apart? They look nothing like each other. I know he'd say that – he's that kind of man.

A LONG STRETCH OF NOTHING IN THE MIDDLE OF NOWHERE

It's a long stretch of nowhere, some say. We drive that way once a week. An hour's drive and we only see two farmhouses. You tend to sit above the speed limit because you see no reason not to. Even the cops drive faster along there. The trees have been stripped from the long paddock, and the regular paddocks are bare and saline. Only at the entries to both driveways are there a few trees, and these struggle. And there's a half-hour's drive between the two. A long stretch of nothing in the middle of nowhere. Everyone says so.

∽

We're hurtling along the road that's a long stretch of nothing in the middle of nowhere, with the stereo up loud. We're listening to the new Megadeth album. The sky is heavy and a storm is expected in the afternoon. It's low ground, and the road often goes under the wash, but storms around here don't usually last long. We are glad we'll be there and back before it hits. An hour there, three hours in town, then an hour back. All done by three o'clock. It looks like the apocalypse, I say, and L comes back with, Yes, mutually assured destruction. After fifteen years of marriage, we don't really laugh at the grimness of each other's jokes, but just nod and accept them.

We are approaching the crossover of the second farmhouse on our route – bitumen to gravel, then about 500 metres before the house and farm sheds. The house is an old colonial mansion, though a little run down now. The machinery, mostly out of the sheds which are being used to hold every bit of hay that can be crammed in, is past its prime. Like many farms in the district, this one is clearly just managing to hold its head above the salt and the drought and the occasional storms and the worryingly low grain prices. In a paddock by the house, some sheep are milling – we always remark that they have the look of either pets or killers about them.

We are almost on top of the scraggly and half-dead trees by the gate when L screams – and I mean screams so loud, Megadeth pales by comparison. Stop stop stop! I hit the brakes and the tyres scream as I struggle to keep them on the road. I see it as the car wobbles and pulls to the left, to the tattered bitumen and gravel road's edge where life can change so quickly if the tyres grip in the wrong way, or fail to grip at all. Watch out! Watch out!

I quickly jerk the wheel to pull the car away from the rough edge, and career into where the oncoming traffic would be, if there were any. The car fishtails and judders to a halt. To compound the implosion of sense, an oncoming car *does* appear and, seeing me and the toddler wandering down the middle of the road, slows and pulls over without too much drama. Within split seconds, our sense of what is what in the world has changed in multiple ways. L and I leap out of our car, as the bloke from his. As we all dash towards the toddler now standing in the middle of the road, we all exclaim at once – What on earth is he doing here!

The child with wispy blond hair is laughing hysterically and running for her life, out into the middle of nowhere from nowhere. My wife calls to me and the other bloke, Stop, stop running after her! Let her settle. We slow down and the child slows down. For some reason I am still not sure of, I stop entirely and the other bloke stops stock-still as well. He and I stand shoulder to shoulder as L walks slowly up to the toddler, who is crying, takes her by the hand, and directs her to the gravel shoulder of the road. Phew, mate, the other bloke said. Unbelievable. Yeah, I nearly cleaned her up. Never seen anyone on the road out here before, let alone a kid, the other bloke says. The toddler looks at the other bloke, then at me, then points at the other bloke, then at me, then back at the other bloke and bursts out crying. L scoops the child up into her arms and rocks her back and forth.

The toddler settles a little and L comforts her, as I swap a few words with the other bloke. I feel overwhelmed by him for some reason – as if he is my soul mate, my brother-in-arms. I feel a kinship in that weird moment. The kid must have come from that house, we seem to all say at once, as if the bloody obvious will bring some relief to the tension. We peer down the driveway and can't see anything or anyone but the sheep. My wife says, She stepped out from behind those trees. Better walk her down to the house.

The other bloke looks suddenly agitated, almost nervous, and moves slowly back a little towards his car. Would you mind, the bloke says, would you mind looking after it all from here? Not much more I can do.

No, not at all … of course we can look after it from here, my wife says. The bloke flicks a quick look in the house's direction, then back at the child, and returns to his car, saying, I mean, they might get the wrong idea, you know, the kid's parents. Whitefellas don't want to understand blackfellas out here. Some of these farmers are real rednecks.

We leave it at that, and reassure him again that we'll sort it, waving goodbye as he drives off. The toddler is restless, so L puts her down. Immediately she tries to make for the driveway, so we cage her in from the road and let her lead the way.

My wife says over her shoulder that she'll take the long trek, and it'll be better for me to sort the car out and then follow them up the drive. So I do that, keeping the car 10 metres behind at less than a snail's pace. The toddler seems happy and marches on, chortling as she goes. L and the child have almost reached the verandah steps of the big house when a woman appears at the open front door. The woman surveys the scene, calmly walks out and down the stairs, takes the child's hand, says 'thank you' and ushers her back up the stairs. Then the woman turns back and says to my wife, It'll storm this evening. Then she makes her way inside and closes the door.

Continuing our drive, disturbed and shaken and silent, we stare hard at the road – suddenly so full of nowhere. Eventually L says, Did you see the mother's eyes? She just stared as if we weren't even there, as if nothing had happened. I add my two cents' worth: She looked as if she was on prescription pills. This annoys L – I don't think so, she says almost bitterly. You're always so judgemental. More like distressed, as if she'd lost the plot and given in. I'm sure there's a real sad story behind that face.

On the return drive, coming back from town hours later, we slow right down as we approach that house, just in case, but there is no sign of life at all. And in the weeks that follow, we always slow down when we go past, but although the machinery has been moved and the hay stack has got smaller, we see no sign of any living thing other than sheep in the paddock.

Now, two months later, we're driving the nowhere road which has become the 'action road' where anything is possible and conversation and silence work intently and intensely hand in hand, and the stereo is never played as it can only form a distraction from our expectations of what might happen. We slowly approach the second farmhouse and notice a *For Sale* sign out front. Actually, three signs. The property is multi-listed and the owners are obviously very keen to sell.

We start conjecturing and can't stop. It's as if two months

of suppression, of pregnant pauses and apprehension, have broken like the storm later on that disturbing day. It had been a storm to remember. Something must have happened to the child ... the woman, I say. Maybe the child wandered off and got bitten by a snake. Maybe it got hit by a car. No, no ... we would have heard, there would have been signs, like the mess a bad storm leaves behind – debris on the road, trees down. Maybe the mother cracked up, or had already cracked up. One of us says that – we're both thinking it. We reach a fever pitch of conjecture then drop it and don't mention it again for ages.

∽

In the weird way that time changes in these parts – going faster and slower at different times of the year, and at different speeds for different people – we find ourselves conjecturing again as we're driving that road. We slow down as always and then L cries, Look, the *For Sale* signs have gone! It's as if something has shifted in our lives. This has again become the road that's a long stretch of nothing in the middle of nowhere. The potential for action has passed. The mother and child are gone from there.

It's as if a load has been lifted from our shoulders. We relax. Even our breathing synchronises. I flip the car stereo. It has been a long time since we've played music on that road. The new AC/DC album. They still rock!

FALLING

It's easy to say there's not a lot to do during the long summer holiday, especially in a mining town too far from the coast to make it a day trip, but it's a fact. Clichés have reasons for existing and usually make sense.

If the kids don't go away to the coast for a few weeks with their parents, they spend their time watching television, playing pool or table tennis in the town hall – which doubles as a youth drop-in centre – or walking up and down the main street, loitering especially outside the deli or the pub with its long cool verandahs.

But what can add temporary interest and occasional piquancy is the influx of two or three city kids, come up to stay a couple of weeks with cousins. They usually don't even last that long, phoning their parents to come and get them, 'it's barbaric up here'. But if they do stay, they get picked on for a while, then become part of the love-hate compulsion of loneliness and isolation. Locals are always hungry for new blood, and the smell of it wards off even the diabolical heat and gets them busy.

These holidaying city slickers usually arrive after Christmas, rarely before, and with their sissy ways and city posing, it's fun to pull them down a peg or two. Strangely, it's almost always boys. Girls rarely get sent out that far, cousins or no cousins, and if they do, they are chaperoned and rarely let out to mix with the feral locals. It did happen once, and Tender Terry screwed the posh bitch on the dust of the sports oval while all the boys watched on, as well as a few of the rougher local girls, and she ended up *up the duff*. Tender Terry had been hauled up by the cops because the girl was fourteen and he was sixteen. Not much came of it, and Tender Terry is now working on the gold mine and screwing prostitutes every weekend over at Kal. He's part of the story of every kid of my generation in our godforsaken town.

As much as we all hate it here, most of us stay on. Even the girls. They get pregnant young and stick around. You need your mum's support, they say. The mines are constantly looking for good workers.

I've always been fairly popular, but there was a holiday-time there when I was about fifteen when things were grim. I was the scapegoat for that summer, as if my ball had come up and I was conscripted as victim to keep things bearable. The victim role usually went to one of the visiting kids from the city – lured in at first with warmth and friendship, eventually to become the rejected, pariahed imbecile. But it didn't work that way that year. And it was a grisly experience with more twists than a barbed-wire fence.

At first I thought we had our gimp for the summer. A pathetic, long, thin streak of a fifteen-year-old wearing glasses, who carried a poetry book around with him. He even read out a poem about daffodils (honestly) to one of the hottest girls in town, one not even Tender Terry had been able to nail. And what's worse, she listened. I said to myself, He's dead meat. We're gonna have fun this summer. It was 110 degrees on the old scale (we weren't that many years into metric then), and lethargy had set in, but this was going to get things rolling, like a spark or a cooling system or whatever. I was excited by the prospect.

And it started off fine. Tender Terry pushed Four Eyes around and warned him off, some of the younger boys in the gang threw rocks and spat at him, and the rest of the girls, the ones we fondly called 'the sluts' because they occasionally roamed the town with us, said he was a poof. He stood up to it for a while, but eventually scurried off into one of the schoolteachers' houses. He was her nephew. We could imagine what the teacher – a new one, so not to be worried about – might have to say to us when school started again.

But then something went really wrong. I had to head down to the city for a few days to visit my Nan, and by the time I got back, Four Eyes was Tender Terry's best mate.

You should've seen 'em, said one of the young boys. They were goin' at Jessie like dogs. Right there in the dirt. First Four Eyes, then Tender Terry, then they both did it again.

And just to make matters worse, I heard: And you should see the length of his cock! It's longer than Terry's!

Tender Terry made it clear to me that I was on the out. I hadn't been there when it counted, seen the Fall of the Hot Chick. It was a glorious moment. And Four Eyes had been the key. He opened her up with his poems, Tender Terry gloated. I'm gonna write poems too, he said confidently.

I noticed Four Eyes leering at me behind his coke bottles as Terry disposed of me: And what's more, you're a boring know-all who doesn't know anything. That was Tender Terry philos-o-phis-ing.

And though they knew I'd sort them out during the next school term, the little bastards of the gang started throwing rocks and spitting at me. Me! The 'ideas man' of their dry little world.

I retreated to the tailings pile by the old mine on the edge of town. I sat there, in the sun, cooking. I found some old corrugated iron, excavated some of the tailings, and put a roof over the hollow. Kept the sun off, though it was like an oven inside. Sat there with bottles of water and moped. In the evenings it wasn't so bad.

My excommunication was absolute, and the triumph of Four Eyes supreme. I heard all the kids had been around to the new teacher's house and had cool drinks and played pool on a table better than the ones in the pub. You've heard of teacher's pets. Well, this was a case of teacher's flock. There was even a rumour that Tender Terry had jumped her while Four Eyes looked on. But I never believed that one.

I kept to myself. I actually made a pretty good place up there on the tailings heap. I insulated it with hessian sacks, I burrowed deep into cooler places. I must confess, I thought if I made it special some of the gang would be curious and come over to my side. But they never did. Not that summer, anyway.

Yet someone did eventually turn up. And we spent a lot of time talking. And, as you know, we're intimately connected these days, but that day we just talked and talked. It was good. She'd be pissed off if she knew I was telling you all this, but it is dry and boring, and long days on the mine do your head in, as you know. Got to let off steam over a few drinks, eh! Got to tell someone your thoughts.

Jessie was no longer the hot girl, or hot chick, but a 'filthy slut'. She wasn't even one of the sluts, who were kind of honoured amongst us boys. She was worse, because she'd been had by *two guys* at once. There were degrees. She was hated by the boys and the girls. Miners twice her age would turn up outside her house pissed and holler for her to come out. Her parents would call the police, who laughed. She was sent to the city for a couple of weeks for counselling and shit. Anyway, one afternoon with the sun peeling skin faster than usual, she found me in my HQ, 'The Hut', out there on the tailings, and we got talking and kept talking. It was boiling in the Hut, but we sweated and drank water and sweated and talked. It was the first real conversation I'd had with a girl. I mean, about serious stuff. Stuff that matters even now, married with kids and a crook back.

I asked her why she did it, and she said, I wanted to fly. To fly out of here. Like on the Royal Flying Doctor when you're sick or smashed up in the mines. I *hate* it here. And Four Eyes's words seemed like they were from somewhere else. Somewhere cool and fresh and full of daffodils. Not scummy plants that live without water and huddle under the sun. But plants that love the sun and reach to the sun because it is comforting. We don't understand what 'warm' is here. It's just hot and less hot. And then he was crawling on top of me and pulling at my clothes and I was falling, falling, and the pain seemed just as it should be, and the dust swallowed me and I suffocated and died.

I said to her, I'll tell you a secret. Don't tell the gang because they'll use it against me. I write poems. I do! Honestly. I just keep them to myself. And they're all in my head. And all about me. I write poems about the dry and the heat and the dust and the tailings and the stunted trees and the hot chick I can't have. But keep that to yourself!

I'd exhausted myself and stared at her. I leant across and pulled a long strand of hair from her eye, wet with perspiration. She moved my hand gently away and said, We are all falling to death. All of us. Even Four Eyes and Tender Terry. They are falling as well, and it's terrible.

EXTREMITIES

Apart from the people, the country is dominated by breakaways, saltbush, mulga, emu bush, heaps of tailings, and active mine sites. In between, there are emus, kangaroos, cattle, sheep, goats, foxes and rabbits. And there are eagles, cockatoos, racehorse goannas, songbirds, termites and echidnas. And much more if you look. Deadly dry or in flood, summer is a cauldron. But the red dirt makes life. You don't have to look hard, though after a while some stop looking. Anything not claimed by mining companies is taken up by cattle stations. It isn't wildflower season. It is mid-summer at the extremities. Tourists stay south.

But it is gold that brings the men to this outback prick on the map, once described by a prime minister's wife as the 'arsehole of the earth'. It is a town of shacks and dongas. The single men's quarters are lined with pick-ups that crunch the dirt, and stone roads branch out to the mines surrounding the town.

The outback is a space of temporary 'fly-in fly-out' homes. Shifting populations go with the mines. Towns don't get a chance. But by local standards this is a very old town and, being on a major highway, it's a stop-off point for truckies, and tourists, in the season. It has its life-thread, though its existence still centres on the mines.

Kepler and Pete were in town on a three-month contract. It was better than being outside town, way off the highway, but it was still six hundred k's from the city, in the heat, and it still meant living in a donga. This time round they were trying to save money to return to Thailand and get stuck into Phuket pussy. They talked about it constantly. Their first visit, also funded by work on the mines, had been a non-stop orgy. Kepler had enjoyed showing the young dog a few tricks, and the young dog's drive kept the old dog on his toes. Kepler was forty and Pete twenty-two, but when it came to pussy, age didn't matter. Except the age of the pussy, of course.

They both worked long shifts, and wanted as little free time as possible. Being there was about earning. On Friday and Saturday nights they drank in the pub, tipping the skimpies, but otherwise they worked, watched pornos on their laptops, and slept. There was a bestiality DVD that did the rounds for a while. Pete and Kepler both watched it (on their own) twice over, and discussed it in detail. Generally, they preferred Asian bondage and black anal. There was a brisk black market for these DVDs among the workers. Helped pass the time.

But when the mine had an emergency shutdown for a couple of days they were at a loss. They started drinking early. Sitting outside the cramped dongas, feet up and hats pulled low, they downed beer after beer, frying in the morning sun. By lunch they were too pissed to care about eating, both enervated and stirred up by the heat.

Pete suggested they go out to the breakaways behind the new mine site. Let's take some beers out there. Kepler agreed, though it wouldn't be any better drinking out there than in camp. But then Pete said, They're full of caves. It'd be cooler in there than out here. Not really deep caves, just hollows in the rock. But they'll be like a fridge. I've been in one when I was a kid.

Driving out, haunted by the stillness, the mines in shutdown, they spotted a goat. Kepler always carried a .243 rifle behind the seat of whichever company vehicle he had. Fuck, Pete, he called, grab the wheel, I'm going to pop that little bastard's clogs.

They tussled between steering wheel and wresting the rifle from its bed. The vehicle skewed across the road, though Kepler had taken his foot off the accelerator. It was still rolling along, vaguely following the goat, which went at a slow trot, looking back over its shoulder. Keep the bloody wheel straight, yelled Kepler. Pete was laughing, near hysterical. Get the little fucker, Kep!

Kepler loved his bolt-action Ruger. He got the barrel out the window and managed to stroke it, load it and fire it with one drunken movement. He winged the goat, which half dropped, stunned, then stood upright and bolted into the scrub.

Got the fucker, Pete yelled. Good shot, mate.

Pulling the rifle in and handing it to Pete, Kepler took the wheel and accelerated. Watch what you do with that, you little bastard. Click the fucking safety on. Which Pete did, because he loved guns.

⁓

They pulled over at the base of a breakaway. They could hear the hot wind crackling through the fluted rock. Grabbing beers, they started lurching up the rock face. As they went higher, they heard voices.

Hear that? said Pete, struggling to grip a rock and hold a sixpack.

Of course I fucking heard it, said Kepler. I wanna see what's going on. He glanced back down. There's a fucking vehicle down there.

He handed his sixpack to Pete and motioned for him to be quiet. He climbed a little higher, peered up, then returned to Pete.

Whoever it is knows we're here, he whispered. Would have seen and heard us miles away. Would have heard that gunshot as well. Probably freaked them out a bit.

As Pete tried to work out the logic, Kepler lifted himself high and called out, Hell-o! Who's up there?

A woman's voice came back, None of your business, mate! Then, after a pause, What do you want?

Kepler, as usual, took the reins. We're from the mines. Day off due to the shutdown. Just going up to the cool of the caves to have a few beers. Warm beers by now!

Pete wondered why they were bothering being careful and polite.

The woman came back after a while with, We're just going.

There was a pause and then she continued, This is Badimia land. Be respectful.

Pete burst out laughing. Fuck, Kep, it's a darkie!

Kepler's racism reached back through generations and he was proud of it, unlike those other racists in camp who claimed they weren't. He said, Shut the fuck up, Pete, you'll scare her off! Let's have some fun. Wonder how many of them there are. Pity you left the rifle in the car.

You didn't say anything about bringing the rifle, Kep.

I shouldn't have to. You should use your initiative.

Seeing Pete downcast, Kepler soothed him. Only pulling your leg, mate. Same sentence for shooting one of those bastards as shooting a white bloke! Did I get you going, mate? Stir your crotch up a little bit? With that, Kepler grabbed Pete's balls and gave them a hard squeeze. Thought so! he said, gleeful. Pete tried, too late, to knock Kepler's hand away. He laughed it off, irritated but used to it.

They reached the caves and looked carefully around. No sign of anyone. They made for the largest one, where their voices echoed. There was ochre painting on the walls. Figures they couldn't quite make out. And emus, roos and echidnas. It was a gallery. Kepler, suspicious by nature, said, No footprints in here. Not even any roo shit. Nothing's been in here for a long while.

Where was that woman when she called out? asked Pete.

Fuck knows. Somewhere *near* here.

They walked out of the cave and scanned the area. They looked down in the direction of the other vehicle but couldn't see it. But the angle was different. Maybe you couldn't see it from there. No sound of an engine starting, of a vehicle crunching its way across the saltbush and quartz fragments to the dirt road alongside the mine.

They drank the beer even though it was hot. It made them pissed and gave them headaches. Crashing on the cool sand of the cave, they stared at the paintings.

That one looks more like a fucking goat than a roo, said Kepler. Must be a roo, though. I mean, these are really old. Probably painted thousands of years before there *were* any fucking feral goats.

Pete half wanted to vandalise them, as a gift to Kepler, because Kepler was talking weird and made him feel uneasy. But he was dizzy and blanked out.

Kepler lifted himself up on his elbow and gazed at Pete. Fucking chip off the ol' block, this one, he said to himself. He looked back at the paintings, which began to swirl and spiral. Shit, must be the heat, takes more booze than that to get me like this. He was in Thailand again, watching Pete arse-fucking a little bitch. Kepler was laughing as the girl screamed, No more, it hurts, it hurts, and Pete went harder and harder. I hate women but I love them, Kep, he'd said after. I have to hurt them to love them.

It was evening when they woke, bursting for a piss. They stood and moaned and unzipped their shorts. Don't piss on the fucking wall, said Kepler. Pete, confused, went out and pissed over the edge, as did Kepler. Pete looked at Kepler's trunk-like dick, full of admiration. Keep your eye on your own pecker, this one's mine, said Kepler. He was out of sorts.

Shit, Kep, look!

Kepler had seen it. Something quick through the rocks.

Looked like a fucking girl!

They ran and slipped and struggled down towards the vision and couldn't see or hear anything. Jesus, like the bloody Nullarbor nymph! said Kepler.

What?

Don't worry, said Kepler, you're too young.

Pete didn't like that. Kepler rarely referred to the age difference.

Gotta tell you mate, this place is giving me the creeps, said Pete.

We should be getting back anyway, said Kepler. I don't have time for a bunch of blacks playing silly buggers.

They woke the next morning feeling really ill. The mine was still shut, and they had little to do but drink and watch pornos. They tended not to squeeze into the one donga to

watch pornos. That didn't seem right in Australia, that was
for holidays – though plenty of blokes did it, especially the
married ones, away from their wives, who seemed to take
comfort in sharing the guilt and the love.

They skipped breakfast, and after hair of the dog, looked
forward to lunch. But the sight of greasy meat piled high
made them want to throw up. They nibbled, green around
the gills, and then left together. The other blokes asked what
had got into them. Can't do anything without each other,
those two. Odd.

Why are we going back, Kep? asked Pete.

Fuckin' think of anything else to do, mate? At least it's
cool up there.

It's cool in the *car*, Kepler, if only you'd wind up your
window and let the air-con do its thing. The vehicle clunked
over potholes left by mining trucks, and they stammered their
*fuck-off*s. Something close to hatred hung in the air. They'd
hit the vodka. Not good out in the heat.

Kepler adjusted the rear-vision mirror and caught a
glimpse of himself. His face was red and weary and he was
getting uglier. Grooves had worn into his cheeks and his eyes
were bloodshot. He glanced across at Pete, still fresh-faced
despite the sleaze in his eyes. He's treading a well-worn path,
thought Kepler, and smiled.

What you smiling at, Kep? asked Pete. Kepler didn't
answer, so Pete, pumped, continued. Might see another goat,
Kep. Maybe I should get the rifle out.

Fuck off. Kepler gritted his teeth. You shoot a goat and
I'll fucking shoot you.

Pete was perplexed. Kepler hated goats. Pete felt he

was with a stranger, and it didn't feel good. He thought of Thailand going wrong. He gazed through the window at the laterite and sandstone outcrops that looked like they'd been chewed and spat out. He never could 'get' this land, though he'd been around it, on and off, all his life. He wondered, if he were stranded, whether he'd eat saltbush and go mad. The sky was so blue it burnt his eyes through the tinted glass, and he turned away, staring down at his jeans.

They reached the cave and flopped on its cool white sand. Pete opened a beer and offered it to Kepler, who waved it away. He was studying the walls.

If you look, he said, you'll see two goats in there among the native animals. Clear as day.

Really? said Pete, who had sculled a can and was flipping open another one. Goats make me want to get hammered.

Kepler turned to him, looked like he was going to hit him, then laughed and took a beer. Pete's spirits were rekindled? On ya, mate. Thought I'd lost you there.

Flaked out on the sandy floor of the cavern, staring at the paintings, they lost track of time. They woke at twilight to the sound of a woman's voice.

Don't drink grog in there, she said.

They looked about them but couldn't see much. It was hazy, getting dark. They had a deadly thirst. Some sort of insects were in the air.

Who's there? yelled Pete.

Only a cicada replied. Stumbling out of the cave and

down to their vehicle, the men were covered in scratches and dry-retching when they reached it.

∽

In his donga, Kepler wakes or half wakes. In his head, he hears women's voices. He gags and searches for water. Cold water. He opens the bar fridge near his bed. Full of beer. Just beer.

The mine will be working today. He pulls on some clothes, and the throbbing in his head gets louder. He wants out. He opens the door and falls through to the dust. The slaughtered goat is strewn over the car bonnet, the windscreen, and through the interior. He gags. It is covered in cicadas, aged cicadas that have emerged from their many years below ground, hiding in the cool before confrontation with the heat. Some of the old blokes at the pub call cicadas the true gold of the town. Take as long as gold to form, and they can fly and sing. More than gold will ever buy you. He remembers this as he reaches past the gore to retrieve his rifle.

Then he calls Pete to come out. Pete appears naked at his door. Kepler eyes him off.

Why, Pete? Kepler asks. Why? Why don't you hear what they're saying? We'll always be tourists, Pete. Even you, and you *come* from this fucking red dust hole, you'll always be a tourist.

What are you on about, you old bastard? What the fuck are you doing with that rifle? Pete notices the remains of the goat. Have you lost your mind? I thought you liked goats these days? Fucking booze sent you troppo?

Your idea of a joke, Pete? Sick little fuck.

Kepler shoots Pete in the genitals, then reloads and shoots him in the head.

Bigoted little prick, he says. No respect for women. I've done the world a favour. Appeased the Goat God. He laughs.

Other miners rush forward, grapple Kepler to the ground and rip the rifle away. He scratches at the red dust.

Now I'm ready to speak with you, you black bitch, he says. No more fucking hiding. Let's have it out, one on one. One on one!

INNER CITY

When Turk and Blue left for the city all their mates said, Watch out, city slickers! And it has to be said that the boys left with every intention of remapping the city, of turning the world upside down.

They were the closest of mates. They had always been neighbours, attended the same schools, and both had lost a parent while young. They played together and drank together; they'd even had sex with the same girl after the school ball.

Some of the townsfolk said they looked like brothers, but that was surely just from almost two decades of always seeing them together. They had grown alike, at least in their mannerisms. Nobody could work out which of them had first got the habit of flicking his hair out of his eyes, even after a haircut when there was not much to be flicked. Nor could it be ascertained who was the first to blow his nose into his hand and then wipe the mucus on any nearby surface. And then there was the knuckle-cracking habit that made even family members want to throw up, and *they* were used to it. Of course, Blue's grandfather was known to do that in his younger days – couldn't much now because he had gout, and his fingers looked like they'd been put through a mangle.

Both Turk and Blue were big strapping lads. The town's older women said that about them with some pride. Fine footballers at school, they'd helped bring the town a couple of trophies. Turk was a ruckman and Blue a forward.

The most startling difference between them was Blue's gingerish-blond hair, though it wasn't really that far in colour and texture from Turk's off-brown blondish mop. If you asked someone from town which was which, they'd seem to forget this difference and say, Well, how can you tell the difference really? It's as if they're twins. An outsider would look, incredulous, and pick it right away, insisting, They don't look anything alike!

Turk and Blue had been talking about moving to the city for a year or more. They wanted a taste of the fast life. They liked going clubbing, and had long been the town's dope dealers. This was kept among friends, though the police and important people around town knew and turned a blind eye. If it wasn't them, it'd be someone worse, seemed to be the consensus. And Turk and Blue did care about their customers, and always kept it basically to mull – didn't want their mates losing it to ice or smack. The odd eckie here and there, but mainly mull. And they grew it themselves, keeping the business local.

That was until they decided to move, and planted a huge crop to dry and package for taking along to the city to sell as the need arose – to finance getting established. They had lined up a small inner-city flat, and they'd play it casual and keep a low profile to start with. Sell a few pounds to mates who'd already moved to the city …

As they drove into the city in Turk's V8 Commodore, which they'd actually both helped buy, they hooted. Whooo-ooo! We're here! We're gunna be mega! Crossing the Causeway, they looked at the skyscrapers and then at the river and said, It looks beautiful. And it was as the evening set in and the sun played out its last tricks on the water. Neither of them was averse to sentimental or even romantic moments. They had layers and layers to them, Ellie used to say. She was the girl they'd screwed together. She loved them both and cried when they left. Don't worry, Ellie, we'll come and visit you.

The flat was furnished, so they only had their clothes and stuff plus twenty pounds of mull. They'd vacuum-sealed the heads in plastic and stacked them neatly in a chest of drawers. On a glass table in the centre of their tiny loungeroom, they placed their prized clay dragon bongs.

Blue says he'll mull up while Turk nips out to get something quick to eat. Neither of them minds cooking, but they haven't had time to shop. When Turk gets back with Chinese they pull a few cones together, though Blue has already had a few. Blue, ya bastard, you could have waited, says Turk, laughing and punching Blue on the arm. Blue rocks sideways to lessen the impact and laughs as well. They are happy, real happy.

And it goes on like that for a few weeks. They get in a

groove. During the day they sleep. At night they go clubbing. A few old mates pop around and Turk and Blue shift a few pounds. They sell it cheap – three thousand a pound. And their punters know the quality. They can live like this for ages. And then why not put in another crop out in the bush back home? Already they are thinking about a bigger place. Already they are thinking about girls who might want to hang with them, rather than just come here after clubbing, smoke their dope in exchange for a fuck, crash out, smoke more in the morning then go. Turk and Blue want more than that in life. They are looking for meaningful relationships.

You guys are pretty weird, says one girl after they ask if she'll screw them both. In bed together. A threesome. We're mates, they laugh, it doesn't worry us. But it worries me, she says. I came home with Blue. But it's not fair, says Blue, the other chick you were with said she was coming, then changed her mind. Where does that leave Turk?

As one might expect, word got around that these country boys had a lot of good mull. Turk and Blue were oblivious to the problems with this, or maybe considered themselves immune, so used to not having to watch their backs because the one was always there looking out for the other. *A lot of good mull.* Bowl always full. The girls they took around to their place spread the word through the clubs. And lots of girls went home with them. A few with big ambitions came back again and again and got really close to one or the other of them, and tried the divide-and-conquer technique – if you want me, then it's time you moved on from your mate. But it never worked. I can tell you now, whatever happens, Turk and Blue remain loyal to each other. There's no flaw in their relationship.

But what does happen is that the word unsurprisingly reaches some of the big dealers in the clubs and they want a bit of the action. At first it's *Sell us a bit of your gear*, which Turk and Blue refuse to do, saying they're not selling (being more than happy with their chain of distribution through old friends). But soon it becomes threatening: *Where do you get this dope we hear so much about?*

It won't be long until we have the cops at our front door, Turk says to Blue. Yeah. Maybe we should shift all the shit straight away? And that's what they do. They sell twelve pounds at two thousand a pound and keep a pound for smoking themselves. The rest has already gone.

You know, Blue, if the cops bust us with a pound we could still go for dealing. That's true, says Turk. I tell you what, I reckon it's time we moved from here anyway. The inner city is pretty boring. Not a bloody tree in sight and I don't know about you, but I am getting pretty sick of clubbing. And Blue, to tell the truth, you've been looking pretty crook lately.

Yeah, Turk, too many eckies and booze. Was much better when we used to stick to the mull. Do you know, we've been here months and we've never been down to the river. I mean, to sit by the river and watch it flow by. We don't do much of anything. And I never thought I'd hear myself say it, but I am bored of fucking these girls who don't give a shit. I miss Ellie.

So do I, Blue, so do I.

And we haven't been home the whole time. We're losing our identity here, Turk. I don't like it.

Nor do I, Blue, nor do I.

And so the boys decided to go out with a bang that night.

We'll visit the clubs, invite all the girls and scaly dealers we've met there, and invite them to our place for an early morning bongfest. We'll blow them out like they've never been blown out before. We'll mull up the entire pound of heads we've got left and leave a smoke haze over the city. If the cops come within a hundred feet of the place, they'll get so stoned from breathing the air they won't know what the fuck's goin' on!

So that's about it, really. Not much of a tale. The party didn't last long because some of the heavy dudes that came with the girls stole the dope direct from the bowls the boys had laid out. They pushed Turk and Blue up against the wall and demanded to know where their stash was hidden. Now, Turk and Blue could have smashed those blokes, but they've never been violent boys. They just said, Sorry, but that's it. All we've got.

The heavy dudes ransacked the place while the girls laughed and the boys laughed with them. Finding nothing, they smoked what dope was left around the table and went off with their ill-gotten gains. By three in the morning, and without too much noise or even too much smoke in the air, the flat was cleared. The boys tidied up the next day, and when they closed the boot on the Commodore and looked back up the stairs to their old centre of operations, it was with a clear conscience. Other than a few burn marks in the carpet, they were leaving it pretty well as good as they got it. They had paid up a few more months' rent so they placed the key on the table and locked the door behind them, leaving a phone message for the real estate agent. Keep the change, they said.

Back home, almost every night for a fortnight, the boys were guests at someone's house, or at a party. Even the shire president had them around for an evening. What are you going to do now, boys?

We thought we might look into setting up house with Ellie.

The mayor, who was no wilting daisy, smiled and slapped them both on the back. That's it, boys, keep it local. You're an advertisement for the town. We all know you could have made it big in the city but you've chosen to come back here. And while you were gone, our young folk went off the rails, you know. Without your guidance we've had all sorts of trouble.

That was the first news Turk and Blue had heard on returning. Speed had come into town through an outsider, and all the kids had gone crazy. A couple were up on assault charges, a good girl on theft charges. Ellie had tried to kill herself with an overdose of hammer. That's what the world comes to when it loses the guiding lights of a generation.

Turk and Blue and Ellie are happy now. The three of them still make a run to the city every so often to move their produce, but all in all, they are homebodies. The boys are coaching the local footy team. Ellie is pregnant, so she has given up smoking and drinking. Turk and Blue tell the tale of the last big smoke-up over and over, always adding that the inner city is not like the rest of the city. When they say this, they flick their hair, and even occasionally blow their nose and wipe it on whatever's handy. I can tell you that they never did this while clubbing in the city. It's a testament to their level of comfort back home. It's where they fit in, and it's where they belong.

THE FAVOURED SON

How did I get this hole through my hand? It's a bullet hole. Bullet went straight through the back of the hand and out of the palm. In and out. True. The evidence is there for you to see. You can poke your finger into the hole. It's sealed in the middle, but you can still tell. That happened twenty-five years ago. Yes, I'll tell you how …

I'd been wandering around the south-west for a couple of years when I came across the Family. I should say right from the beginning that this was what they called themselves, and what they were known as in the tight-knit orchard town of Z. It wasn't a religious thing – well, they were religious – strict Catholics – but I mean, it wasn't like a cult or anything. They were all related – all close family – just part of what we might now call the cliché of the hard-working Italian migrant family. Two generations who came out together in the late fifties and kids who were born in the early sixties and on. From scraps of land they built up orchards and market gardens in no time – the whole family labouring from sun-up to sundown when the kids weren't at school. They mixed with other Italian migrant families, and fought to keep their values. Out our way in the central wheatbelt, we saw a few Italian families – a lot more Slav single men who had come out to do the clearing, and stayed single in their tin and asbestos huts on forty acres, all their lives. We – the *old* farming families – didn't get on well with the 'Eyetie' kids at school, truth be told. We used every name we heard from our own for them, and others we invented. We used to joke that they only ever drove red Dodge trucks, which was pretty ridiculous considering my dad had a Dodge truck.

So I arrived at Z and started asking around for work, as I usually did when I arrived in a new town. I had my swag and a few dollars left from the last orchard I'd worked in. I went straight to the front bar of the pub, ordered a beer, and got chatting to the barmaid. She told me they were looking for hay carters out at the Family's place. I looked sidelong at her and asked if it was a religious thing, of course. Nope, that's just our name for them. They stick close together. Then, for no apparent reason, she said, Vince – that's Vincenzo – is a spunk. That was more information than I needed, but to make matters worse, she continued, But Lou – Luigi – would be a real catch. Got his head screwed on right. He's gonna be rich like his old man – like Papa.

The Family's property was a bit out of town, so I tried to hitch a ride in the direction the barmaid had told me. It wasn't a big town and there was only a road in and a road out, so it was easy enough. And it didn't take long for me to hitch a lift. It was much easier since I'd shaved my dreadies, I can tell you. Looking for work, mate? asked the old bloke who picked me up. Yep, I said, and before I could continue: 'You'll be heading out to the Family's place, then …? Yep, I said, and that was the sum total of our conversation.

He dropped me off at the gate. White-painted wooden posts all the way down to the house. An orange orchard off to one side. A large milking shed. Plenty of spring pasture. Grapevines, olives, apple trees. A newish brick house – maybe ten years old. Out back, a smaller weatherboard place – the original house, no doubt. A dog raced towards me, barking and going at my ankles. A red cloud kelpie. It was getting late in the day, so I was taking a gamble that they'd want me and that they'd let me stay on the property. I guessed the old house was empty – the sort of building they'd keep for workers, I told myself confidentially. I could hear cows in the shed – milking time.

An old lady covered in black came out through the front door, yelling at the dog, and then yelled at me in broken English. It was just like in my childhood. I wasn't sure if what I felt was prejudice, or something about being out of place. Strange really, as so many of the people I'd worked for in my wanderings had been Italians. So many apples and pears and oranges picked in their orchards. I got on well enough with them, if keeping my distance. Mind you, they kept their distance from me, too. And it's a truism – if you're a hard worker, the Italian boss will like you well enough. And I am a hard worker. More than once in the past I'd heard it said from one boss to a neighbouring boss, Don't let the hair fool yer, he's a bloody hard worker, and reliable. I've always been proud of that.

So as she yelled at me, I called back, shaking the dog off my boot, Hi, I was told you might be looking for workers. Yeah, yeah! the old woman replied, reaching to grab the dog by the collar. She shouted at it in Italian, and the dog took off for the milking sheds, stopping briefly to look at me over its shoulder and growl. Dogs can always tell something about you you'd rather pretend wasn't true.

Sure enough, Papa installed me in the old house. The old lady – Nonna – Papa's mother – brought me the best food I'd eaten in months. And yes, it was pasta with homegrown tomatoes, olives, the works. And a bottle of wine.

I was ready to go at dawn, though I wasn't called for until later – the cut hay was a little damp from the morning and it's never good to bale with too much moisture in the grass. It was Vince who collected me. I could tell – as the barmaid said, a 'spunk'. Or what, back at school, would have been called a 'homo'. He was dapper in his work clothes, and kind of rocked as he walked. Hair rolled in waves. His belt buckle was large, and it gleamed. Astonishingly, he wore braces as well as the belt. Bright blue braces. Slick as. He spoke in a strained Aussie accent: How ya goin', mate ... you gonna be helpin' us out over the next couple of weeks ...? Lot of balin' to do. Lot of work. When I'm finished, I'm up to the city for some partying. I chatted with him as we walked to the hay sheds ... he was a clubber. He asked if I smoked dope. He asked if I took speed. He told me his life's history. Heart-on-his-sleeve kind of guy. That was Vince.

At the sheds his brother, Lou, was waiting. Crisp in his fleecy checked shirt, sturdy workboots, shearers' greasies. Hair short and neat, nothing out of place, nothing extra, not a touch of affectation. There was a family resemblance, sure. But they weren't two peas from the same pod. Lou shook hands and said it was good to be working together. That he was looking forward to it. And you could believe him. I liked him. But then I liked Vince as well. And Nonna. And Papa, though I hadn't really swapped more than a few gruff words with him. And then there was Mamma. I'd seen her out of the corner of my eye – I guess you'd say a stylish-looking woman in her late forties. Papa looked about fifty-five. The Family. By proxy, I already felt part of it.

The days rolled by, as they say. It was good hay-carting weather, though as anyone who has done the job will know, there's never a perfect day stacking and restacking bales of hay. Your skin is a hell zone and every muscle in your body aches. But the boys had style. After baling, Lou drove the truck while Vince and I took turns at taking bales off the loader as it scooped them from the ground, swinging them to each other, to stack on the truck bed. It took skill to build a pile of blocks at the rate Lou drove – he expected the work to be done steadily and efficiently – and Vince's joking and singing at the top of his voice made the time pass all the quicker. And then we had to stack the shed when the truck was fully loaded. All three of us at work. Two in the shed and one on the truck hurling bales down, then up, as the stack built. Though I'd done the job plenty of times before over the years, I still picked up some good hints from the boys about how best to roll the bales and stack them neat.

Throughout the day, Papa would come down from the house to watch our work. He was up well before daybreak with an assistant who lived in town – a dairyman – to bring in the cows and do the milking. When they weren't carting or doing some other work in the orchard, the boys would be in with the cows as well. Same in the evenings. But Papa still found time to make sure everything was going fine. He'd test our handiwork on the truck – poking at the bales to ensure they were secure, commenting if Vince had let them go a layer or two too high – you'll lose the lot, you'll lose the lot, he'd repeat. Actually, he seemed a bit hard on Vince. There was clearly stuff between them – issues – but I kept out of it. I once heard Papa screaming at him about being lazy. Vince wasn't lazy – he was just, well, 'free'. I smoked the odd scoob in the evenings with Vince, but he said to keep it from his brother because he'd tell Papa who would throw us both out. Believe me, he added, if an Italian son can get thrown out, then it's bad news!

There was only two weeks' work, and at the end of it Lou gave me my pay and my marching orders. You've been a good worker, mate, he said. That was it. Vince was slightly emotional and we went into town and the pub that night and got pissed. Vince screwed the barmaid out the back of the pub somewhere, and I held the pool table for five games. One of Vince's old schoolmates gave us a lift back to the farm, since both of us were too out of it to drive. We walked down that white-posted drive with a full moon overhead, arm in arm, singing our lungs out. We didn't even know the words of the songs. Whatever came out would do. The dog barked and barked and pulled against its chain. Cows bellowed in the distance and the porch light came on. Lou and Papa came out and yelled, as one, for us to keep it down, we'd wake the women. But there was nothing more to it – hard work brings a little bit of slack, even in the Family. Vince said goodnight and lurched off to his father and brother, and I slunk into the old hut.

The next morning, I started to get my shit together and get ready to head off. I went up to the house to say thanks to Nonna for the fine food I'd been eating, and to thank Mamma, who had generally kept away from me. She didn't fraternise with the hired help, I'd say. But she was warm in her thanks and her goodbye, and Nonna gave me a hug. I stood at the back door the whole time – I'd never once been into the main house while I was there. I saw Christ on a crucifix on a corridor wall, but that was it.

By that time, the milking was over and the cows were being led back to the paddocks. I went to say goodbye to the blokes. Vince was in the shed, washing it out, looking worse for wear, and just gave me a sickly grin and a lacklustre wave. Papa was taking the cows down to the paddock, but I'd see him shortly, because he'd promised to drive me back into town when I finished work, and to introduce me to a friend who was looking for someone to help with some fencing. Papa said to me, You'd make a father proud … I will recommend you to my old friend Joseph. We came out on the same ship as boys. He will be a good boss for you.

I couldn't see Lou anywhere. I went to the hayshed. I walked around the tractors and truck. No sign. I went back to the hut. I opened the door and Lou jumped back from my pack. His rifle was leaning against the wall. It all looked really weird.

What? I said.

Sorry, Lou mumbled … I thought you might have some …

Some what? I asked, closing the door behind me.

He just repeated, Some, some, then changing his mind and demeanour, went across to his rifle. There's a sick cow. Papa wants me to shoot it. I hate shooting cows. It's down in the yard behind the dairy. I hate it. Papa knows I hate it and he makes me do it. He says it will toughen me. That I will be head of the family one day. That Vince isn't responsible enough. He never makes Vince shoot the sick cows.

I was speechless. I was looking for some grass, he said. Some marijuana. I know you smoke it with Vince. I always know. I know what Vince does. I thought it might make it easier. Easier to kill the cow, you know.

It won't make it easier, Lou – it will make it harder, if anything. I grew up on a farm, as I've told you. I killed lots of things and never liked it. Swore I'd never do it again.

I've gotta, said Lou. There's no choice. I've gotta.

So I blew Lou out, and Lou got silly, then sick, and I knew there'd be trouble. I knew before I rolled the joint. I knew I'd be excommunicated, that I wouldn't be working for Joseph.

Papa will be back soon, I said to Lou. Come with me.

I picked up his rifle and led him swinging back and forth out of the hut down to the dairy. I could hear Vince still swishing away and we sidetracked around to the holding yards. The sick cow was actually a fair way from the dairy. It was a walk through manure and slush.

I'm not going to do it, Lou half cried and half laughed.

Neither am I, I insisted.

Lou snatched the rifle off me and buggered around with the bolt. Somehow he loaded it.

Don't swing it near me, I said.

He started to aim at the cow then lowered it again. Nope, I don't care what Papa thinks, I'm not going to do it. And it doesn't even make sense. It's not good business. That cow could be saved by a good vet. Just because the old methods haven't worked, doesn't mean modern medicine couldn't bring it around! It'd be good business to save it.

The gun swung about all over the place as Lou staggered around, raging. By this stage, Vince had abandoned the hose and was standing nearby, watching on, hands on hips, a wry, almost gloating smile on his face. I reached to grab the rifle, to eject the bullet from the chamber. Then we heard Papa yelling at us from across the paddock. I wasn't even sure what he was saying. Lou looked up, panicked, wrestled an imaginary figure with the gun, and it discharged.

That was twenty-five years ago. I could have been a rich man out of it. Papa offered me a huge bribe to keep my mouth shut. Mamma wept and threw herself on me. Nonna offered to nurse me forever. But I didn't want anything. My head was crowded with the vision of Lou clutching remorsefully at my bleeding hand, while Vince strolled over, lifted and reloaded the rifle, and shot the cow.

A SEASIDE BURIAL

Estranged though they'd been, the family – most of whom had hated the dead man, their father and grandfather, even more vehemently than they did their mother – turned up to see him buried. The 'new' wife of thirty years mourned with real tears; the ex-wife who hated him turned up with her entourage, reinforcing them reinforcing her, still the Queen. And then there were the great grandchildren and their hangers-on, who stalked and lurked like a murder of crows.

At that time of year, the sea was choppy and grey. And that was on an azure blue coast when for most of the year it glowered. Yet with this grey it wasn't being mournful but more honest – heavy metals and other pollutants just swirling around in the mix, silt of dredgers emptying the river's mouth, the harbour, of its poison residues, out into the deep, to be swept back onto the shores. Gulls were raucous. They will be, right to the end.

One of the small children, innocent of the hell brought to the occasion by the embittered 'family past', worried that the sea might come up over the sand, up this hill, and into the cemetery. It might wash great-grandfather away? Don't worry, said an aunt, dressed in trendy black with witchy lacework, the fish won't be interested. Nothing tasty there. The girl stared at her aunt, whose midriff showed, G-string eating into bare thighs, and wondered what would happened if she pinged the string. She was a distractible kid.

The widow didn't know where to stand, closed in by a semicircle of hostility, until an in-law went and stood by her: a tall, angry-looking man, husband of the 'black sheep' daughter. Don't worry, he said, J (the 'black sheep') will be here soon – she's just parking the car. And sure enough, a minute later, the ominous cliffs broke apart and J walked through. Her family, her *real* family, stared hard at her, trying to penetrate the foreignness. It's that terrible man she's with, they whispered. He's like Dad, Pop … They hung in the breeze, which was blowing steady from Antarctica now, cold with winter. They hung like seagulls. Or maybe birds of prey hanging over the hanging seagulls. Less likely, they were scavengers for souls and didn't believe the father's dead body was going to yield anything up. What had been left was taken by *that woman*, the widow. But they felt good knowing that, though they'd never visited before, they'd driven hundreds of kilometres inland to go through his possessions while she was delirious in the hospital. They were helping her.

J's man was an enigma. He didn't speak with them. Who does he think he is? they asked. All of them had heard whispers. He'd been a drug addict, once, and always had a runny nose (they were sure – they'd rarely ever seen him as J never appeared at family picnics, and even though she wasn't specifically invited, should have had the fortitude to ask when one might be on). He wrote pornography and called it literature. They shuddered as one, and drew their children close. The Queen, struggling with her gold lamé top, sniffed in the widow's direction and said loudly, These occasions are about *family*! She nestled into her brood, who knew J's man was a clear and present danger.

The service was brief. J and the widow had chosen some music, but it wasn't played. Old family favourites crackled over the PA and the Queen said loudly, Remember this, kids? He hated it so much! They looked solemn but smiled inside. It was good to feel warm on such an unpleasant day, weather-wise. Parents instinctively glanced down at the ocean, and at the great swathes of sandy beach, which, despite being blocked off in places by new Tuscan Splendours, looked inviting even in this weather. One thought: I'll still squeeze into that bikini this summer … Another thought: The tailor will be running soon, be nice to get down there with some of the boys from the office (how rare it is for an office of blokes to share the same interest) … I could wear my new overalls and parka. He thought fashion worked everywhere. That day he wore a tasteful off-the-rack suit that looked designer, with a muted blue tie. His father always overdressed – those bright suits were unbecoming – and spoke like an ocker. Women should dress brightly, not men. His mother had taste.

The Queen thought, Well, *she'll* get the house – and I got to carry all the babies.

And then the funeral celebrant struggled to give a potted history of the deceased's life; said he was going to a better place, and that one had in mind those he'd left behind. He then requested any last words. The widow sobbed and looked around. One of the dead man's sons recounted a story of his own childhood that was about a great time out he'd had with his parents, then corrected himself by saying, Actually it was only with his mum because his dad was away travelling as usual. He finished by saying: He was a flawed man.

The celebrant begged for anyone to say a word. Silence. J was too distressed, and tried to comfort the widow. The Queen sent burning hot eyebeams in her errant daughter's direction, but J could only think how the rising and falling of her tears and those of the widow blended with the waves crashing against the beach, dissolving into memories of her father.

The tall man stood up and went to the lectern. I have something to say ... I knew Bill pretty well in recent years and he and I got on fine. He was a witty bloke who loved his footy team, the Sharks. He told a good yarn.

As he spoke, the family sent a tempest his way. They willed flames and death. They invented monstrosities and perversities they were sure he had committed. They burned to be outside so they could share their epiphanies. It struck all of them, as one body, young and old, how much the tall man looked like their father when he was young, when he was theirs, when they didn't want him and knew he was a bad man. He's a bad man a bad man a bad man! And then as the tall man babbled on and on, droning like the waves, the body-of-family felt suddenly relaxed, like pissing in a cold sea and feeling briefly blissfully warm inside one's bathers. The Kraken had been awoken. The Leviathan had emerged again. Their father had been reborn and this time he wouldn't escape their punishment. They were happy, and had the ocean to thank for it. Whose idea was it to bury him by the sea anyway? They all glanced over at the Queen, who loomed large as a thunderhead rising up over the ocean. They felt glad that her thunder and lightning were no threat to them, that it would always be directed towards mariners coming from strange lands carrying their cargos of unpredictability.

And they only half heard the tall man say: And though he thought of himself as an inland man, loving the great wheat crops and even the blank pitiless areas of salinity, he always talked of the sea, of raising his children within earshot of the waves. He used to say to visitors, See that shell over there on the mantelpiece, lift it up and you'll hear all my kids and their mother laughing and playing on the sand, the water bluer than blue, the waves gentle but interesting. And what's more, if you hesitated, Hilda, his second wife and dedicated partner of thirty years, would generously say, Go on, go on … take a listen … it makes him so happy when you hear who he is!

ACKNOWLEDGEMENTS

Agni, Westerly, The Literary Review, Meanjin, Story Quarterly, The Reader, The Kenyon Review (online), and *The Kenyon Review.*

John Kinsella's most recent volume of poetry is *Jam Tree Gully* (WW Norton, 2012). His collection, *Armour*, won the 2012 Victorian Premier's Award for Poetry. His most recent volume of stories is *In the Shade of the Shady Tree* (Ohio University Press, 2012) which was shortlisted for the Steele Rudd Award. He is a Fellow of Churchill College, Cambridge University, and a Professorial Research Fellow at the University of Western Australia. He is poetry editor of *Island*.